Hopeman's Legacy

When Leopold Hopeman bequeaths his fortune to the towns-folk of Little Creek, they use the money wisely and found the prosperous Hopeman Town. But with the booming settle-ment attracting men who want only personal gain, Mayor Tucker hires former Pinkerton detective Nimrod Dunn to find out why the fortune is now being squandered.

Nimrod soon uncovers the likely culprit, but his investiga-tion takes a strange twist when he learns that Mayor Tucker has a dark secret and that he might not be the benevolent man everyone thinks he is. With Nimrod both carrying out an investigation for the mayor and at the same time investigating him, he'll need all his cunning to uncover the truth while staying one step ahead of the many guns lining up against him.

Hopeman's Legacy

I.J. Parnham

A Black Horse Western

ROBERT HALE

© I.J. Parnham 2019
First published in Great Britain 2019

ISBN 978-0-7198-3011-2

The Crowood Press
The Stable Block
Crowood Lane
Ramsbury
Marlborough
Wiltshire SN8 2HR

www.bhwesterns.com

Robert Hale is an imprint
of The Crowood Press

Typeset by
Derek Doyle & Associates, Shaw Heath
Printed and bound in Great Britain by
4Bind Ltd, Stevenage, SG1 2XT

PROLOGUE

'If nobody has anything else to say, we should raise our glasses to a great man,' Clayton Jones said. He looked around the small gathering in the Hard Trails saloon. His wife, Jessica, shook her head, while Trinity Tucker was facing the coffin that stood on a table in the centre of the saloon room.

As the other two people, Wallace Hall and Alexander Caldwell, had already said a few words about Leopold Hopeman, Clayton started to remove his hat, but then Trinity turned to him.

'I reckon I ought to have the final word,' he said.

'Please do,' Clayton said, taking a step backwards to let Trinity stand beside Leopold's coffin.

Trinity moved forwards and placed a hand on the coffin before turning to face everyone.

'A month before Leopold's untimely demise he came to me.' Trinity withdrew an envelope from his pocket. 'He'd made a will. I don't know the details as he only talked about his intentions, but this might be the right moment to open the envelope and read it.'

Trinity waited to see if anyone objected, but he received only affirmative grunts.

'Go on,' Clayton said.

With a sombre air Trinity opened the envelope and shook out the two folded sheets of paper within. He scanned the first page and confirmed it provided the same instruction as the one Leopold had spoken about during their meeting before looking over the top of the paper at everyone.

'I, Leopold Hopeman, have no kin,' he said, paraphrasing the long-winded legal jargon. 'I view the townsfolk of Little Creek, the small place with a big heart where five years ago I settled down to enjoy the quiet life, as being my closest friends. So I want my legacy to be shared equally amongst everyone here.'

'He was a good man,' Clayton said.

'One of Little Creek's finest,' Wallace said.

'I'll always remember him fondly,' Jessica said.

Then a reflective silence reigned until Alexander asked the obvious question.

'What has he left us?' he said.

His question made Wallace mutter under his breath about its inappropriateness, but Clayton and Jessica looked at Trinity with wide eyes, which suggested they were as eager to know the answer as

Alexander was. While trying to keep his expression stern to avoid revealing his own interest, Trinity turned to the second page.

He read the details and then blinked before reading them again. He hadn't been mistaken and so, using a voice that broke several times, he read aloud.

'I, Leopold Hopeman, bequeath to my friends in Little Creek my legacy of two hundred and fifty—'

'He's given us two hundred and fifty dollars!' Jessica said. She pointed at each person in the room while counting. 'There are five of us, and I may not be good with numbers, but I know that's fifty dollars each, and that sure is a welcome gift.'

While everyone voiced their approval of her statement, Jessica picked up a whiskey bottle from the counter and set about recharging glasses. Then everyone raised their glasses to take a drink, but Trinity coughed, drawing their attention back to him.

'You should have let me finish,' he declared. He paused, and then began reading again. 'I, Leopold Hopeman, bequeath to my friends in Little Creek my legacy of two hundred and fifty *thousand* dollars.'

Jessica uttered a high-pitched squeal; Alexander downed his whiskey in a single gulp; Wallace dropped his glass; and Clayton stumbled into the coffin, making it rattle on the table.

7

'Thousand?' Clayton said, his voice gruff with emotion. 'Did you say "thousand"?'

Trinity tried to reply, but his mouth had gone dry and he could no longer form the words, so he held out the sheet of paper. Clayton took it off him and read it, and then, rubbing his brow, passed it on to his wife.

When everyone had read the details, the sheet was returned to Trinity. Everyone stood rigidly while staring straight ahead, so he tucked the will back in the envelope. A minute passed before Jessica broke the frozen tableau by picking up the whiskey bottle to fill the empty glasses, but her hand shook so much she couldn't pour even one drink.

In the silent room she put down the bottle and leaned over the counter. She stood hunched over it for a while, then started giggling. The giggling grew louder until Clayton laughed, and that encouraged everyone else to show their surprise with whoops of delight, clapping, and huge grins.

Then the party started.

CHAPTER 1

Five years later

'We'll meet up outside the office,' Sydney Jones said. 'Don't go inside until I get there.'

Sydney received curt nods from eight of his men before they moved off in pairs. Nimrod Dunn stayed with Sydney to watch how they fared.

Two pairs walked beside the train, using the deep shadows in the middle of the night to stay hidden. The other two pairs headed past the cattle pens with their heads lowered, ensuring that the noise from the pens and the poor light kept them from being noticed.

When everyone reached the office, Nimrod and Sydney moved on. Unlike the others they took a direct route, walking across ground on which there were patches of light. This meant they might be seen, but Sydney had confided in Nimrod that for his plan to succeed they needed to be noticed. When they reached the door the man who was usually the first to raise objections, Reed Goodwin, gestured at him.

'You told us to be careful, but you sure weren't,' he whispered. 'One of Alexander Caldwell's men could have seen you.'

'I want there to be witnesses,' Sydney said and then raised his neckerchief to cover his mouth and nose. 'But don't worry. I also want to get away before anyone can catch us.'

'Then you're a fool, and I'm not doing anything more you say.'

Sydney pointed back along the way they had come.

'In that case stand aside and let us sort out your problems for you.'

Reed shook his head, but when the other men gave no sign they would back him up, he adjusted his own kerchief and turned to the door.

'Let's get this done before someone comes,' he said with a weary air.

Sydney slapped his back, and then with a gesture that ordered the men to follow him in, he put a shoulder to the office door. The door clattered open with such speed it had clearly not been locked, so Sydney stumbled on for two paces until he could stop himself.

Reed and two other men surged in after him – but then Alexander Caldwell spoke up from inside.

'It's the middle of the night, but what can I do for you?' he said with a light tone.

'It's a trap,' Sydney spluttered. 'Get out now!'

Nimrod turned around, only to find that armed men were emerging from the shadows with their guns aimed at them.

'Too late,' Nimrod called. 'This is over.'

Sydney's men still bustled out of the office, but they were unarmed, so when they saw the forces that were aligned against them they raised their hands. Then their only course of action was to troop into the office to face the gloating Alexander.

When Sydney's men had been lined up, Alexander sat down on the front of the desk facing them and his gunmen took up positions around the office. Alexander didn't speak until everyone had lowered their kerchiefs.

'I pay a fair wage for an honest day's work,' he said. 'So there was no need for it to come to this.'

'You sure don't pay a fair wage,' Sydney said. 'You're exploiting us.'

'My business is successful because of my hard work. If you're not prepared to work hard, I don't reckon Caldwell's Stockyard is the right place for you.' Alexander snorted. 'So what did you plan to do? Wreck my office?'

'We did, and if you don't accept our demands your problems will only get worse.'

11

Alexander stood up and walked along the line of workers before returning to stand before Sydney.

'I employ hundreds of men. There are ten of you. You don't seem to have much support.'

'I have more men than this.'

Alexander took several moments to respond, presumably to let Sydney register his mistake.

'So who else is involved in your attempted sabotage?'

Sydney shook his head. 'You're not getting no names.'

Alexander frowned and looked at Nimrod, who returned his gaze blankly. From the corner of his eye Nimrod noted that Sydney glanced at him, having clearly noticed Alexander's look towards him before he dismissed the matter with a shrug.

Alexander turned to the gunmen who were nearest to the door.

'Take these men away. The train leaves at sun-up, so keep them entertained until then. When they're far enough away from Black Creek, throw them off.' Alexander pointed at Sydney, Nimrod and Reed. 'These three will stay to answer my questions.'

The gunmen led the workers out of the office, receiving no opposition from the men, who had accepted they were beaten.

'I'm not telling you nothing,' Sydney said when his men had gone.

'I'm sure your resolve is strong, but what about these two?' Alexander stood before Reed. 'Give me some names.'

'Sydney's boasting,' Reed said with a sigh. 'He struggled to get anyone to listen to him, and most of us wouldn't have joined him if we'd have known his full plan.'

'That's an interesting story.' Alexander moved on to stand before Nimrod. 'Are you, too, going to claim that only Sydney wanted to be seen wrecking my office?'

Alexander shouldn't have mentioned Sydney's plan, as Nimrod had given him this information in confidence, so Nimrod thought quickly and then shrugged.

'Reed told the truth,' he said. 'Sydney could only recruit a ten-man team.'

Alexander jutted his jaw before moving back to Sydney, but Sydney ignored him as he again looked at Nimrod.

'Alexander was waiting for us,' he intoned, his slow speech showing he was thinking aloud. 'That means someone sold us out.'

'Maybe someone did, but it wasn't me,' Nimrod said. 'Alexander must have heard us talking about your plan when we were outside.'

'We spoke quietly, and you was the only one I told beforehand that I wanted witnesses.'

Nimrod murmured a denial, but Reed snarled with anger and advanced on him. Nimrod stood his ground, so Reed shoved his shoulders.

Nimrod rocked back. Then Reed aimed a round-armed punch at his head.

Nimrod jerked away so the fist caught him with only a glancing blow to the cheek. Then he moved back to confront Reed, which led to one of Alexander's men stepping forward and grabbing Reed's shoulder.

Reed twisted to the side and freed himself, but that made Alexander's man aim his gun at Reed's chest. Reed still advanced a pace, but then sense overcame his anger and he contented himself with gesturing at Nimrod.

'This isn't over,' he said, his eyes blazing. 'I'll make you pay for this.'

Nimrod considered trying to protest his innocence, but he doubted he'd be believed. He straightened up.

'I was just doing my job,' he declared. 'I'm a Pinkerton detective.'

Reed's shoulders slumped as this revelation appeared to knock the fight out of him.

'I guess I ought to be flattered,' Sydney said. 'I'd never have thought a few workers grumbling about their lot in life would have warranted hiring you.'

Nimrod turned to him. 'It was worse than that. If

you'd carried out your sabotage the stockyard could have descended into chaos and lost thousands of dollars.'

Sydney took a few deep breaths, and when he spoke his voice was low and defeated.

'Maybe it would have, but as you've heard everything that we've said, and seen everything that we've done, you know the sabotage was my idea, and nobody else was involved.'

Nimrod faced Alexander. 'He's right. There's no need to question anyone further. The nine men you caught are the only malcontents, and I can give you a report on their activities.'

Alexander nodded and then ordered one of his gunmen to take Reed away. Despite Nimrod's successful plea for clemency, Reed still glared at him and he struggled so much a second man had to take hold of him, after which he resorted to abuse and threats as he was dragged outside.

'So report,' Alexander said, when Reed could no longer be heard.

Nimrod set his feet wide apart. 'You suspected that an organized group was planning to disrupt your operations, but it was just a few workers grumbling, like all workers do. If Sydney hadn't stirred up that discontent you wouldn't have had any trouble, and if you'd dismissed him as I suggested, it wouldn't have got to this stage.'

His final comment made Sydney mutter under his breath, but Alexander pointed at Nimrod.

'I didn't ask for your opinion. Who else will give me trouble?'

'I don't reckon anyone else will have the guts to cause problems. Once the word gets out that you've dismissed some men, that'll be the end of it.'

'You're not listening to me,' Alexander snarled. 'I don't want your opinion. I want facts.'

Nimrod took a pace forward, his irritation with Alexander's attitude growing.

'In that case, the facts are that your workers are right to be annoyed. You pay them less than they deserve, and they put in more effort than you deserve.'

Sydney clapped his hands, making Alexander cast a warning glare at him until he stopped. Then Alexander paced back and forth while rubbing his jaw.

'Or it could be that you didn't find all the troublemakers.'

'If there are any, I won't find them now.'

Alexander stopped pacing and nodded. 'Then we're of the same mind – that you're not the right man to root out all the dissent.'

'I meant that after you made me reveal my role, the truth is sure to get out.' Nimrod tipped back his hat as he looked at the glowering Alexander. 'But that's not important, as I quit.'

Nimrod hadn't thought about his declaration beforehand, but his heart thudded rapidly with the assurance that it was the right thing to do. Alexander's only reaction was an unconcerned shrug.

'You can't quit because I'm firing you.' Alexander turned his back on him and faced Sydney. 'Now leave us. Sydney and I have some business to discuss.'

CHAPTER 2

Hopeman Town was as promising as Nimrod had hoped it would be. He was one of around twenty people who alighted from the train and melted into the crowd that thronged the main drag. People bustled everywhere, all seemingly having a purpose. New buildings surrounded him, while other buildings were being constructed on both sides of the rail tracks.

As he walked along he smiled, and the dark mood that had overcome him in Black Creek started to lift. Earlier that day, after deciding not only to stop working for Alexander Caldwell but also to resign as a Pinkerton detective, he had boarded the train into which Sydney's associates had been bundled. He hadn't seen them again.

He didn't know where he would go and what he would do next, but on the journey he recalled the good things he'd heard about Hopeman Town. And based on his first few minutes, he reckoned he'd made a good decision to come to this town. So he leaned against the corner of a building and surveyed the scene – and that let him notice a problem.

Reed Goodwin, who had threatened him in Black Creek, and his colleague Pablo Rodriguez were walking behind him, but when they saw him looking their way they slipped into an alley beside a stable. Their actions could have been innocent, but he took no chances and set off back towards the station.

When he reached the stable the men weren't visible, so he leaned against the corner of the building and kept one eye on the alley. The men didn't return, but Nimrod now reckoned he would stay in Hopeman Town for a while. As he didn't want to postpone a potential problem, he walked down the side of the stable.

He peered ahead, but the first sign of trouble came from behind. A faint footfall sounded around ten paces away, presumably from someone trying to follow him quietly. Nimrod showed no sign he had heard the noise, and was halfway along the wall when he again heard a footfall. This time it was only a few paces behind him, so he stopped and swirled round.

Sure enough, Reed was sneaking up on him and had raised his arms as he prepared to grab him – but as soon as he was noticed he stopped three paces away.

'It seems you've come to Hopeman Town, too,' Nimrod said with a light tone.

'I didn't have a choice,' Reed said, lowering his arms. 'I lost my job in Black Creek and I was kicked off the train here.'

'After the threats Alexander made, you got off lightly.'

'I did, but only for one reason.' Reed took a pace forwards. 'Everyone got a beating before they were thrown off the train and nobody knows what happened to Sydney, but I was spared on the promise I'd deal with you.'

'You're angry, but don't make the mistake of taking me on. I have some experience of these types of situation.' Nimrod gave him a disarming smile, which only made Reed scowl. 'I'll offer the same advice to your colleague, wherever he is.'

Reed winced and glanced past Nimrod, suggesting Pablo could be making his move.

'What colleague?' he asked.

Nimrod was too experienced to fall for that trick, but, feeling almost sorry for Reed and his unsubtle attempt to engineer a sneak attack, he put his back to the wall and half-turned his head so he could watch him while looking for Pablo.

As nobody was visible, he turned back, but a shadow flitted on the ground and that alerted him to the fact that someone was above him. With a quick movement Nimrod threw a hand to his holster, just as Pablo leapt from the flat roof of the stable.

Despite Nimrod's quick reaction, he had yet to touch leather when Pablo caught the back of his right shoulder and knocked him forwards. Both men went down, with Nimrod landing on his chest and his assailant slamming down on his lower body.

Nimrod's chin crunched into the ground, rattling his teeth. With him incapacitated Pablo grabbed his arms from behind and dragged him to his feet.

Nimrod shook himself, and when he'd regained his senses he was facing the grinning Reed.

'You're not the only one who can be sneaky,' Pablo muttered in his ear.

'Lying in wait for someone is easy,' Nimrod said. 'Learning what Sydney Jones was planning without being discovered is sneaky.'

'If you're trying to talk your way out of this, you've failed,' Reed said.

'I was just making clear what went on in Black Creek. I was hired to expose Sydney. If you want to blame anyone, blame him for getting you into this mess, and blame yourself for following him.'

Reed glanced at Pablo, suggesting it had been a good idea to mention his disapproval of Sydney and his tactics, but Pablo snarled and shoved Nimrod forwards.

21

'That's enough talk,' he said. 'You're just hoping someone will come along and help you.'

Reed nodded and bunched a fist as he moved closer to Nimrod.

'I agree, except it won't work,' he said.

Pablo had been right that Nimrod had been playing for time, as he'd seen two men stop at the end of the alley. With the possibility that an alarm could be raised soon he thought about other ways to distract his captors, but then Reed launched a swinging blow at him.

The punch slammed into his chin and knocked him back against Pablo, who stood his ground. Reed then hammered a backhanded blow to his cheek that knocked him to the side.

Then the blows came quick and fast to his body and face, and Nimrod could do nothing other than put up with it.

'My turn,' Pablo said after a while. 'You can't have all the fun.'

Reed grunted that he agreed, and moved to take control of their captive. Nimrod went limp and let his head and shoulders loll to make it harder for them to transfer him. Sure enough, when Pablo released Nimrod's arms, Nimrod dropped to his knees before Reed could get a secure grip of him. Nimrod reckoned that was the best chance he'd get, and he twisted to the side while getting to his feet.

Then he launched himself at Reed. Unfortunately the blows he'd received had weakened him and he managed only a faltering step, but then he saw the reason why he'd managed to get free with relative ease. Both men were ignoring him as they looked down the alley towards the main drag. A moment later a strident voice rang out.

'Step away from him!'

Reed and Pablo glanced at each other. They both nodded and turned away as they prepared to take flight, and that gave Nimrod enough time to kick the back of Reed's right leg, making him stumble.

While Pablo ran on, Reed swirled back round with his fists bunched, but then he appeared to dismiss the matter and set off after Pablo. Nimrod broke into a run after him, but he could only stagger along and he soon came to a halt.

While his tormentors scampered around the back of the stable, he turned to the two men who had interrupted the altercation. One was smartly dressed with a stove hat and lively eyes, while the other had a gun aimed at the end of the stable.

'And now?' the armed man asked his companion, who pointed in the direction Reed and Pablo had fled.

'I presume they arrived on the train, and it leaves shortly,' the man said. 'Impress upon them their need to be on it.'

The armed man nodded and stalked off.

'Do you need any help?' Nimrod called after him while slapping his holster.

The man looked over his shoulder at him and snorted a laugh before carrying on. Nimrod watched him until he'd disappeared from view, and then smiled at his other saviour.

'Don't concern yourself with Buck Garrett's welfare,' the man said. 'My bodyguard knows what he's doing, and the only men in danger are your attackers. I assume that doesn't worry you.'

Nimrod rubbed his jaw, seeking out sore spots before poking his ribs. He figured he'd been saved before he'd suffered any serious damage.

'They reckoned they had a legitimate grievance, so I hope they take the hint and leave town.'

'Your attitude does you credit.'

'As does yours. You not only stepped in and helped me, but you haven't asked what the altercation was about.'

The man spread his hands. 'I don't need to know the details. I can quickly ascertain a man's character, and I know you'll make a fine addition to our town.'

Nimrod shrugged. 'Then you know me better than I know myself, as I don't know how long I'll be here.'

'In that case you can buy me a drink to show your gratitude, and while Buck completes his mission I'll persuade you to settle here.'

The man gave a beaming smile that was so open it made Nimrod laugh.

'I can already see you're a persuasive man.' Nimrod held out his hand. 'I'm Nimrod Dunn.'

'And I'm Trinity Tucker, one of Leopold Hopeman's closest friends and a founder of this fine town.' Trinity took Nimrod's hand and shook it. 'I'm now the mayor, and that means I'm the man who'll make all your dreams come true.'

CHAPTER 3

'I don't have a dream,' Nimrod said when he and Trinity were standing at the bar in the nearest saloon.

'Every man has a dream,' Trinity said. 'Hopeman Town is where they become real.'

'This is a decent town, so it could be a good place to work out what my dream might be.' Nimrod fingered his whiskey glass and decided to confide in Trinity even though he hadn't asked any personal questions. 'I was a Pinkerton detective. I resigned.'

'That must have been a big decision.'

Nimrod sipped his whiskey. 'In the end it wasn't. Lawmen hold the line between right and wrong, and men like Buck protect good men, but my assignments weren't so clear cut. I often had to bring down men who were more decent than the men who hired me, even if two of those victims then tracked me down.'

Trinity clinked his glass against Nimrod's.

'I'm impressed that this worries you even after a beating.'

Nimrod shrugged. 'You shouldn't be. It's taken me years to leave, but my last assignment at Caldwell's Stockyard broke me. I had to expose workers who were organizing a strike. Except their grievances were valid, they probably wouldn't have withdrawn their labour, and Alexander Caldwell deserved to suffer.'

Nimrod would have provided more opinions about Alexander, but Trinity tensed up when he mentioned his name. Then Trinity swirled his whiskey and leaned towards Nimrod.

'Alexander was an old friend of mine,' he declared. He set his stern gaze on Nimrod, and then winked. 'Except these days I wish that double-crossing varmint a lifetime of misery.'

Nimrod sighed with relief. 'Are you saying he was once different?'

'I am, and the change involves a tale I had intended to tell you.' Trinity gestured to the bartender to top up their glasses, and then led him to a table where he sat opposite him. 'How much do you know about Leopold Hopeman?'

'Nothing, other than I assume he had something to do with the town that bears his name.'

Trinity sighed before he adopted a level tone that

27

showed he'd told this tale many times before.

'He did, although that was after a career building railroads. When he came here the settlement was only a few buildings huddled around Clayton and Jessica Jones's saloon. Most people had moved to Black Creek, but Alexander Caldwell, Wallace Hall and myself stayed. We welcomed Leopold, although we didn't know about his past. Clearly he enjoyed that.'

'He sounds like a modest man.'

Trinity nodded. 'We only found out he was wealthy after he died and left us his fortune. It was so much money we didn't know what to do with it.'

Nimrod gestured at the window and swept his arm to the side indicating the whole town.

'I assume you built all this.'

Trinity frowned. 'We did, but at first the money brought out the worst in Alexander. Leopold speci-fied it should be divided equally, but Alexander reckoned that as Jessica and Clayton were married they should gct only one share and that as I hadn't lived here for long I should get less. Not surprisingly, his suggestions would have resulted in him getting a larger share.'

Nimrod snorted a laugh. 'That sounds like the Alexander I worked for.'

'To stop the arguments I suggested creating a fund to make our town prosper. Alexander disagreed, and the arguments were so heated Clayton Jones became apoplectic with rage. Then he collapsed and died. After that we gave Alexander a quarter of the money to stop his complaints, and he left to start his stockyard, while the rest of us carried out my plan to fund businesses, as well as a school and a hospital.'

'Your philanthropy has clearly worked.'

Trinity smiled. 'And your use of that word means I was right to encourage you to stay. All you need is a dream, and the Hopeman Legacy Fund will finance your business until you succeed.'

Nimrod frowned. 'And it's that easy, is it? I suggest an idea and you give me money?'

Trinity raised his glass and looked at his whiskey as he chose his next words carefully.

'Obviously it's not that easy. At the start we trusted people to treat us with respect. Many did, but others cheated us. Now we're more circumspect. You give the fund a half of your profits until you can afford to repay your loan.'

'And if I can never afford to do that?'

'Then the fund loses, but the town is prospering, so we make more good decisions than bad ones.' Trinity glanced at the door where Buck had just returned. He nodded to him and turned back to Nimrod. 'Buck has now dealt with your problem, so if you work out what your dream is, see me and we'll discuss business.'

29

Trinity downed his whiskey and scraped back his chair, although he stayed sitting as he awaited a response.

'If I have an idea I'll take up your offer, but I doubt I will. Being a Pinkerton detective is all I've ever done and I can't see what else I could. . . .'

Nimrod trailed off and looked aside as an idea that perhaps ought to have been obvious came to him.

'What's just come to mind?' Trinity asked.

'I'm a good detective, and I only gave it up because I hated my assignments, but if I worked for myself I could choose my clients.'

Trinity nodded. 'That's a great idea. This town doesn't have a private detective. Even better, you won't need a licence or much money. I'll get someone to see you, and by sundown you'll be ready to start your first assignment.'

'I'm obliged for your help, but I reckon it might be a while before I get my first client.'

Trinity stood up and leaned over the table to smile at him.

'You're wrong. You already have one.' He tapped his own chest and then withdrew a watch from his vest pocket. 'But time is pressing, so I'll explain later in your new office.'

With that, Trinity shook his hand and then headed to the door, pausing several times to exchange pleasantries with customers. When he joined Buck he

30

spoke with him, and that made Buck look at Nimrod, his gaze lingering on him before he and Trinity headed away.

Nimrod nursed his drink, and when the mayor's aide arrived, to his delight Trinity turned out to be as good as his word. So at sundown he was standing in front of his new office looking down the main drag at what would be his first assignment.

The office was five paces wide and nothing more than a storeroom for the next-door mercantile that was no longer being used, and into which a desk and chair had been placed. The window was a slit in the front wall that barely let in enough light to see, and the door opened on to a side alley, although that meant the office would complement his clandestine activities.

Those activities would start soon, because when Trinity visited late in the afternoon he had tasked him with investigating the Excelsior theatre. The Hopeman Legacy Fund financed anyone with a viable business venture that would help the town prosper. Most of these ventures were like Nimrod's and required only a small outlay, but some ventures were larger, and in the case of the Excelsior theatre, were too large to risk failure.

Trinity and the other fund managers, Jessica Jones and Wallace Hall, had accepted the need for this enterprise to add prestige to the expanding town,

31

but so far they hadn't seen a return. The suspicion was now growing that Lawrence Saunders, the theatre owner, was taking advantage of them. Nimrod had accepted the task without the reservations that had marred his most recent assignment, as Trinity was clearly a decent man and it was likely Lawrence was not.

As people were now gravitating towards the saloons, Nimrod figured this was a good time to consider the scene, so he headed to the theatre. He had expected it to be popular in the evening, but everyone was streaming past the open doors, and when he reached it he saw the reason.

A playbill on the door announced that the theatre would next be open on Saturday, five days from then, when it would present a play entitled *Hopeman's Legacy*. A smaller notice said that Haywood Milton's acting company was looking to cast a part in the play, so with that offer giving him an excuse to go in, Nimrod headed inside.

Nobody was looking out for visitors, so without being challenged he slipped into the auditorium, where he found that a rehearsal of the play was in progress. Nimrod sat on the fifth row where he watched proceedings. He hoped to get a clue about the personalities of the gathered people and to overhear something useful, but all he learnt was that Haywood Milton was in charge. The five actors, four men and a woman, just followed Haywood's instructions and moved around the stage while speaking their lines.

They repeatedly enacted one scene involving a heated argument, and each time Haywood declared himself unsatisfied with some aspect of their performance. But without a context for that scene, Nimrod couldn't work out what the play was about.

The bemusing activity led to him looking around the auditorium, and he formed his own theory about why the theatre was unprofitable. The seats were firm and plush, gilded statues of actors in dramatic poses were beside the stage, gleaming lamps adorned the walls, and even the ceiling had ornate carvings of people and animals. Clearly no expense had been spared for this prestigious building. Yet it wouldn't be earning money until the weekend, and then it was presenting a play that, from the title, might have local interest but which didn't sound interesting.

After an hour, Haywood declared a break in the rehearsal and the actors settled down in chairs on the front row. Haywood also jumped down from the stage, whereupon for the first time he appeared to notice Nimrod and came over.

'Do you like my play?' he asked when he'd sat down beside him.

'To be honest I couldn't work out what was going on,' Nimrod said.

'But hopefully you've been intrigued enough to return when the play opens.'

'I had a different motive for being here. I've just arrived in town and I read your notice outside.' Nimrod smiled, but Haywood furrowed his brow. 'You're looking for an actor.'

'Ah, I'm afraid that notice is old and I now have everyone I need.' Haywood rubbed his jaw. 'Although I could use an understudy.'

Nimrod considered responding with enthusiasm and then finding out later what this role would entail, but he decided that in his new endeavour he would use as little subterfuge as possible.

'What's an understudy?' he asked.

'It's a common enough term for. . . .' Haywood frowned. 'Have you had much experience of acting?'

'None, as such.'

'In that case I'm afraid you're not what I need.'

Haywood stood up and moved to leave, but Nimrod raised a hand halting him.

'I haven't acted before, but I'm a detective, so I have plenty of experience of pretending to be someone else.'

'Then I'm sorry. You're still of no use to me. Being able to pretend you're someone doesn't mean you can make an audience believe you're a fictional character.'

'I disagree. If an actor fails he gets booed off the

stage. If I fail I could get shot.'

Haywood laughed. 'Getting shot for bad acting isn't unusual in some of the places I've been, and that bruise on your jaw suggests you're not as good at what you do as you think you are, but I hear your point. I'll consider your offer and get back to you.'

Nimrod thanked him. Then, with Haywood heading back to the stage, he reckoned he shouldn't appear over-eager and stood up to leave, but on a whim he called after Haywood.

'What's your play about?'

Haywood turned to him and gestured extravagantly.

'It's the tale of the birth of this town, which everyone has heard a hundred times, except not in the way I'll present it.'

Nimrod glanced at the actors who were awaiting Haywood's return and then hazarded a guess.

'You have five actors, so are they playing Mayor Tucker, Alexander Caldwell and the rest?'

'They are, but we still have much to do before they can convince everyone they are these people.'

Haywood clapped his hands and then bounded on to the stage while calling out for his actors to gather around him.

As the rehearsal restarted, Nimrod moved off. He didn't know if Lawrence Saunders was in the building, but figuring that he'd made enough progress that day, he resisted the urge to explore the rest of the theatre and headed outside.

The mayor's aide had booked him a room at one of Jessica Jones's two hotels, with the first three months' charges being added to his loan, but before going there he returned to his office to lock up. He was glad he did this, as the door was ajar. There was nothing inside worth stealing, but he still back-handed the door the rest of the way open and looked into the gloomy interior.

A thin stream of light coming through the window let him see that Reed Goodwin and Pablo Rodriguez were leaning back against the desk. They weren't looking his way, but Nimrod saw no reason to delay what was probably another inevitable confrontation, so he stepped into the doorway, making them turn to him.

'I thought Buck Garrett told you to leave town,' he said.

'He did,' Reed said. 'We didn't.'

'Then you're fools.' Nimrod rubbed his side to give the impression his bruises still troubled him while using the movement to place his hand near to his holster. 'I have no problem with you, and you have nothing to gain by harassing me.'

'We're not here to harass you.'

Reed glanced into a dark corner of the office and a moment later Sydney Jones stepped into view.

'They work for me now,' Sydney said. 'And once I've explained myself, so will you.'

'We didn't part company in Black Creek on good terms,' Nimrod said. 'So why should I do that?'

'Because you're a detective and I have a job for you.' Sydney sneered. 'I want you to investigate Mayor Tucker, a man who makes that double-crossing piece of slime Alexander Caldwell look like a saint.'

CHAPTER 4

Nimrod walked into his office and closed the door behind him. When he'd lit an oil-lamp and set it on his desk, he faced Sydney.

'First you had a problem with Alexander,' he snapped. 'Now you have a problem with Trinity.'

'I only have a problem with the man who killed my father,' Sydney said. 'I thought that was Alexander Caldwell. Now it would seem it was Mayor Tucker.'

'I didn't know that,' Nimrod said with a more conciliatory tone. 'I assume that explains your activities at the stockyard.'

'I *was* trying to bring down Alexander, so I'm grateful you stopped me ruining the wrong man.'

Nimrod moved closer to Sydney and looked him over.

'When I left Black Creek it looked as if you'd be lucky to get out of that office alive, except I'm more bruised than you are.'

'I accused Alexander and he accepted my reasoning for my activities. Then he told me his side of the story. I believed him.'

Nimrod blew out his cheeks in surprise.

'Why did you trust him?'

Sydney conceded his scepticism with a sigh.

'It helped that he released me without reprisals, but I'm keeping an open mind about him, which is why I want you to get to the truth about what happened to Clayton Jones.'

'So Clayton was your father,' Nimrod mused. He thought back to the story that Trinity had told him, and then nodded. 'I've heard about some of the events of five years ago. Clayton got into an argument with Alexander, and he got so worked up he keeled over and died.'

Sydney gave a slow and sorry shake of the head.

'That's the official story, but I gather he was a calm man, so he sure didn't die in no fit of rage.'

'I assume your mother accepts that Trinity's version is right, so talk to her about it.'

Sydney frowned and walked away from him, as if he was working out how he should respond.

'Jessica isn't my mother,' he said when he returned. 'When I was a child Clayton abandoned my real mother to go off with her, a saloon girl.'

Nimrod winced. 'I guess the rest of this story is

that despite Clayton dying a rich man, none of that money has been passed down to you.'

'I gather that Trinity's contract for the fund is watertight.'

'Then I can see why you're annoyed, but it's still a big step to conclude that Trinity killed your father. So what did happen?'

Sydney blew out his cheeks, and then raised and lowered his arms in a display of being exasperated.

'Alexander doesn't know. At the time he was in Black Creek working on a deal to open a stockyard. When he returned Clayton was already dead, and it was much later before he heard that Trinity was spreading the story that Clayton had died during an argument with him.'

Nimrod shrugged. 'That's the kind of lie a guilty man might make, but there could be other explanations. Either way, this isn't my problem, as I've already accepted an assignment from Trinity.'

Sydney gave a wide smile. 'Then you're ideally placed to get close to him and find out the truth.'

'Perhaps I am, but I'm no longer a Pinkerton detective. I now work for myself. That means I only work for clients I like, and I reckon Trinity is a good man whose generosity created this town.'

Nimrod met Sydney's eye, letting Sydney gather his unspoken implication as to why he was not accepting his assignment, which he acknowledged with a shake of the head.

'I said Nimrod can't be trusted,' Reed said. 'He was in Alexander's pay in Black Creek, and now he's in the pay of another rich man.'

Reed and Pablo both advanced on Nimrod with menace. Nimrod stood his ground, but Sydney raised a hand.

'Leave him alone,' he said. 'If he talks to Trinity, it'll suit my purpose for him to be worried.'

Reed firmed his jaw, looking as if he wouldn't back down, but then with a shake of the head Pablo turned to the door. Reed directed a last warning glare at Nimrod, and then followed him.

'I won't tell anyone you were here,' Nimrod said to Sydney.

'And I won't interfere in your investigation.' Sydney shrugged. 'Although when I expose the darkness behind Hopeman Town's pleasant false front, take care it doesn't bring you down with it.'

Nimrod nodded and backed away, giving Sydney the last word. Sydney still dallied before he followed the others to the door.

Reed and Pablo stepped outside – and then both men swirled round to look towards the back of the building with a surprised expression on their faces. Reed twitched a hand towards his holster, while Pablo opened his mouth to say something.

Then a gunshot ripped out. Lead slammed into

Pablo's chest, making him take a staggered step backwards and ensuring that only a pained screech escaped his lips.

Reed drew his gun and blasted lead as another gunshot tore out, this time hammering into Pablo's forehead and toppling him. As Sydney hurried to the door with Nimrod at his heels, Reed was trying to scramble for safety, but another gunshot cracked and he dropped to his knees clutching his side, then keeled over in the doorway.

Sydney grabbed his shoulder and dragged him into the office, and Nimrod joined him to help – but when they laid Reed down on the floor, blood was spreading across his chest and his eyes were glazed.

Nimrod glanced at Sydney and shook his head. Then, with his gun drawn, he edged up to the doorway and glanced outside. The light in the alley was poor, but it was strong enough for him to see along its length. The gunman wasn't visible, so he turned back to Sydney.

'Stay here while I deal with this,' he said.

'You're not doing this alone,' Sydney said as he drew his gun.

When Nimrod nodded they slipped outside. With Nimrod walking beside the near wall and Sydney hurrying to the other wall, they moved towards the source of the shooting.

When they reached the end of the alley Nimrod

looked around the corner of the office, but again he didn't see anyone. Sounds of consternation were increasing behind them as the gunfire had alerted the townsfolk. Nimrod edged past the corner and peered ahead at the open ground, then to either side at a line of buildings, all with back doors, along with alleys into which their quarry could have made good his escape.

'I'll go this way,' he said when Sydney came out of the alley and saw the scene for himself. 'You try in the other direction.'

Sydney nodded and moved off. Nimrod watched him until he had checked out the first doorway, and then moved on. He ran behind his office and the mercantile, and then past two more buildings until he reached the back of the theatre, but then he stopped as there was a wide gap between the theatre and the next building, a stable.

He craned his neck to look around the corner of the theatre towards the main drag. Twenty yards ahead a man was walking away, his form indistinct as he passed through the shadows by the wall, but his gait was slow as if he didn't expect to be confronted.

Nimrod followed, matching the man's steady pace. The man would have to walk through a pool of light before he reached the main drag, so he reckoned he would then get a clue as to his identity.

The man was just about to enter the light area

when in a moment he disappeared from sight. Nimrod blinked, figuring this development was a trick played by the interplay of light and shadows – but the man didn't reappear, and within moments Nimrod closed on the spot where he'd last seen him.

Nimrod stopped and peered at the lighter patch ahead, and then at the inky darkness beside the wall, the light leaving behind ghost images that ensured he couldn't work out where his quarry had gone. Then all at once there was a rustling sound, and a hand was slapped over his mouth from behind.

He was dragged towards the wall. His assailant was strong, and he was pulled further than he expected, so the man must have been hiding in a recess. Then a sharp object was jabbed into his side, presumably a gun.

Nimrod jerked his elbow backwards, catching his assailant in the ribs and making him grunt. With the sharp object no longer sticking into him, Nimrod squirmed and managed to free himself – but only for a moment, as the man crunched a blow into the back of his neck that sent him sprawling on the ground on his front.

Nimrod twisted round to look up. He couldn't see his assailant, but he caught the glint of gunmetal and the gun was aimed down at him.

He tried to raise his own gun, but the blow had jarred his senses and he struggled to move.

Thankfully the man held his fire, and with each passing moment Nimrod discerned more of him, seeing first his arm and then the outline of his body.

He was surprised at how quickly his eyes were becoming accustomed to the dark, but then he realized it was the light level that was increasing. Then the recess was flooded with light as a man arrived holding a lamp aloft, letting Nimrod see that his assailant was Buck Garrett.

'Have you caught him, Buck?' someone shouted behind him.

'No,' Buck said. 'This one had nothing to do with the shooting.'

Buck glared at Nimrod and then relaxed his gun arm in an apparent acceptance that he'd accosted the wrong man. But the stern set of Buck's jaw made Nimrod think that only the fortunate arrival of a witness had saved him from being shot.

Buck then headed back towards the main drag, using the same slow walk he'd adopted before. Nimrod rubbed his brow, and with a shake of his head decided he was now feeling fine.

He got up to watch Buck leave. Then he moved on to join the witness.

'What made you look down here?' Nimrod asked after he'd introduced himself and learned he was talking to Hubert Latham.

'I thought I saw someone lurking around,' Hubert

said. He gestured towards the dark shadows by the stable. 'Though I was starting to think I'd been mistaken. Then I came across you two. Clearly in the dark Buck thought you were the shooter, so you were lucky I came along when I did.'

'I guess I was.'

Nimrod peered around, but other than the people who were gravitating towards them to see what was happening, he didn't see this other man or anyone else acting suspiciously enough to be the shooter.

When Hubert left to explain to the others what had happened, Nimrod watched Buck until he headed into the nearest saloon. Then he explored the area where Hubert reckoned he'd seen someone, but he failed to find anybody or anything of interest.

When he returned, Sydney was walking towards him shaking his head, so Nimrod explained he'd been checking out Hubert's tenuous and possibly erroneous sighting of a man in the shadows.

'So it looks like he got away,' Sydney said.

'Perhaps not,' Nimrod said. 'Hubert wasn't sure what he saw, but I reckon I know who did it, except there were no witnesses, and I can't prove anything – and I doubt anyone would believe me anyhow.'

'Who do you think it was?'

'Buck Garrett was strolling away from the scene, and he probably would have killed me if Hubert hadn't come along.'

Sydney winced. 'If the mayor's bodyguard is shooting up people without fear of recrimination, you have to accept I'm right, and that there's a darkness in Hopeman Town.'

'I do.' Nimrod rubbed the back of his neck and smiled at Sydney. 'So I guess that means I'm now working for you, too.'

CHAPTER 5

'It's clear what happened,' Marshal Walter Farr said when he'd heard Nimrod's side of the story the morning after Pablo and Reed had been killed.

'Is it?' Nimrod said. 'You don't know who shot them.'

Farr shrugged, and then left Nimrod's office to stand on the patch of ground where Reed and Pablo had been shot. He cast a cursory glance in the direction where the shooter would have been standing, and then faced Nimrod through the doorway.

'People like them aren't welcome in Hopeman Town, so I'm not surprised they annoyed someone.'

'I gather Buck Garrett told them to move on.'

Farr nodded. 'I've already interviewed Buck, and he's sure you didn't do it.'

While shaking his head in bemusement, Nimrod joined Farr outside.

'That's mighty generous of him, seeing as how the most likely reason he's sure of that is—'

'Choose your next words carefully,' Farr snapped. 'I don't want to hear unfounded accusations against a man who's an asset to this town.'

'I wasn't going to make an unfounded accusation. Buck was walking beside the theatre coming from the direction of this office. He heard me following him and accosted me.'

Farr lowered his head as he appeared to give the matter some thought. When he looked up, he nodded.

'That supports what Buck told me. He heard the shooting and looked down this alley. He saw two dead men and you giving chase. So he headed to the side of the theatre to look for the shooter, and met you.'

Nimrod rubbed his jaw as he considered the merits of pointing out the inconsistencies in their stories. He hadn't seen anyone looking down the alley, he hadn't run, and Sydney had left the office with him, but as Sydney had asked him not to mention his involvement, he only shrugged.

'If you're sure that neither Buck nor I did it, you still have a killer to find. I'd suggest you talk to Hubert Latham, as he saw a man lurking around.'

'I hadn't heard about that. I'll follow it up.' Farr frowned. 'But I doubt I'll ever find a culprit. Anyone could have done it, and I have plenty of other matters to deal with.'

Farr nodded to him and moved off. Nimrod watched him leave and then called after him.

'I know you must be busy,' he said. 'Everyone tells me this is a peaceful town. It's a credit to you and your diligent work.'

Farr stopped and looked back at him with narrowed eyes as he presumably wondered whether Nimrod had been sarcastic. Then he dismissed the matter with a thin smile and walked on.

Nimrod headed back inside and sat at his desk. Presently, Sydney slipped into his office.

'What did the lawman say?' he asked.

'He doesn't know who killed them, but he's sure it wasn't Buck,' Nimrod said.

Sydney snorted. 'In short, he doesn't care.'

'That sums it up, and you don't sound surprised.'

'Unlike you, last night I didn't sleep in one of my stepmother's grand hotels. I stayed in the place she used to run outside of the main town. It's now Oliver Peak's lice-ridden hole, and I heard the opinions of people who haven't prospered here. It made interesting listening.'

Nimrod raised a hand. 'I want to keep an open mind, so I don't want to hear those rumours.'

'You can investigate in any way you want, as will I.' Sydney slapped his holster.

'It sounds as if we'll work well together, with you on the outside and me on the inside.' Nimrod frowned. 'Or at least I'll do that when I can get close to Trinity, along with Wallace Hall and Jessica Jones.'

Sydney nodded. Then they agreed on several neutral locations where they could meet, along with a few signals to exchange information secretively.

When Sydney left, Nimrod headed to the saloon where he and Trinity had enjoyed a drink together the previous day. He had received a description of Wallace and Jessica, but they weren't there, and neither was Trinity.

He moved on. In addition to her hotels, Jessica owned three saloons, so he worked his way through them. In the third one, the Long Night saloon, he found two of the people that interested him, Wallace and Jessica, along with Haywood Milton. They were sitting at a corner table and chatting amiably. On the table was a bulky sheaf of papers, presumably Haywood's play, which suggested the subject of their conversation.

Nimrod ordered a drink at the bar while he considered how he could use the opportunity that had presented itself, but then found he didn't need to, as Haywood saw him and waved him over.

'Do you think he's suitable?' Haywood asked Jessica and Wallace when he'd sat down at their table.

51

Both of them peered at him. Wallace frowned, but Jessica gave a slow nod.

'He's too young, but he has the right build,' she said.

'Only if you're not paying attention,' Wallace said with a snort of contempt. 'He's a terrible choice.'

Jessica opened her eyes wide while meeting Wallace's eyes.

'This is the man we talked about last night. You should give him a second look.'

Wallace sighed. Then he did as he'd been asked and looked Nimrod over.

'I was right the first time that he's too different, but I can see why you like him. So on second thoughts he does have a quality that means he's suitable.' Wallace shrugged. 'Not that he'll have to do anything.'

Jessica turned to Haywood. 'That's Wallace's way of saying he approves of him as much as I do.'

As Wallace murmured something under his breath, Haywood slapped the sheaf of papers and beamed at Nimrod, as if he should have been able to work out what they'd just discussed and so share his delight. When Nimrod didn't respond, he turned to Jessica.

'I'm pleased,' Haywood said. 'Being a likeness is unimportant, but being able to project the essence of a person is. After all, the actress playing you doesn't have your beauty, but she does have your charm.'

The flattery made Jessica simper and Wallace groan, but Nimrod smiled, having now picked up on a potential explanation for their discussion.

'Do you now have a role for me in your play?' he asked.

'I do,' Haywood said, turning back to him. 'I have five actors to play the principal parts, but I hadn't originally intended to include the sixth and most crucial person, Leopold Hopeman.'

Nimrod rubbed his jaw. 'Your play is about the birth of this town, and that happened after he died.'

'I know. I want you to play Leopold's dead body. Do you reckon you can do that?'

Nimrod chuckled. 'It'll be a challenge, but I'll do my best.'

Jessica laughed, but Haywood nodded knowingly.

'It will be. I had intended to have a coffin on stage, but a body will provide a more dramatic focus for the story and that means you'll have to lie still on the floor for two hours.'

'Then I hope you'll advise me on how best I can perform my role.'

This time Jessica stifled her laugh, but again Haywood didn't appear to find anything humorous in Nimrod's response as he nodded and then looked at Wallace and Jessica in turn.

'It appears that everything has been agreed to our

mutual satisfaction. You approve of my actors and my little play.'

'The actors look nothing like us,' Wallace said grumpily. 'None of the events happened, and nobody ever said any of the lines you've written, but as you keep telling us, the truth isn't important.'

'Exactly,' Haywood said. He dragged the sheaf across the table and hugged it to his chest. 'This play rips apart the well-known facts and rearranges them into a form that delivers a more fundamental truth, one that'll resonate with the audience and make them question whether in your place they'd have had the wisdom to make the same decision.'

Wallace sighed. 'On that basis I don't suppose I can complain.'

'And you have my support,' Jessica said. 'Trinity is a busy man, but we spoke with him last night and he had no objections.'

Wallace shook his head, suggesting Trinity hadn't offered any supportive comments either, but Jessica again looked at him with wide eyes, so he stood up without making any more unenthusiastic comments.

'I'm delighted,' Haywood said. 'So I'll look forward to seeing you all on opening night.'

'I'll try to stay awake until the end,' Wallace said.

'He really is looking forward to Saturday,' Jessica said as she joined him in standing up. Then she looked at Nimrod. 'And I'm looking forward to seeing you play a dead man. If you need any information about the man you're depicting, seek me out. You'll find me in one of my saloons during the day.'

'And in the room above yours at night,' Wallace murmured under his breath, although he probably spoke louder than he'd intended to, as Jessica shot him a harsh glare.

'I'm sure I'll have questions,' Nimrod said, making her smile before she and Wallace headed to the bar. He watched her leave, and then turned to Haywood. 'And thank you for giving me a part.'

Haywood dumped his play back on the table and frowned.

'I was being diplomatic while they were here. The truth is, I couldn't get anyone else to do it.'

Nimrod laughed. 'According to you the truth isn't important, not that I understand what that means.'

Haywood glanced around checking that nobody was close by, but he still lowered his voice.

'You've met some of them. Trinity is a politician who says what you want to hear. Wallace is a cynic who wastes away his life at the bar. Jessica is a flirt who craves the attention of men even after the death of her husband, a passive and uninteresting man, unlike the aggressive Alexander Caldwell.'

'Are you saying that if you'd portrayed them as they really are, they wouldn't have approved your play?'

Haywood nodded. 'Even with my flattering versions of them they've questioned my decisions, but that constraint forced me to look for the better truth, one that only a story can deliver.'

'That in the end they used a dead man's generosity to build a town?'

'That's right, and I could only write that by leaving out the messy irrelevancies.'

Nimrod didn't reply immediately, to avoid showing how much this comment had intrigued him.

'What type of messy things?' he asked with an amiable tone.

Haywood fingered through the top sheets of his play before settling on an answer.

'The main events were the discovery after Leopold's death that he was wealthy, Trinity's proposal that they should build a town, the arguments that resulted in Clayton's death, and everyone agreeing to Trinity's plan.' Haywood raised a finger. 'But those events happened over many months, and that's dramatically inconvenient. So I've made them happen in one scene after the discovery of Leopold's body.'

Nimrod gave a supportive nod. 'I can see that'll make the play easier to follow.'

'It will be. Nobody is interested in the extraneous information. The facts just confuse.'

'But still, those events are still facts. Leopold was

wealthy, Trinity did propose building a town, and Clayton did die.'

'They are, and by concentrating on those elements and ignoring the rest, I've distilled the chaos into a compelling drama.' Haywood patted the sheaf. 'If I'd included such things as this not being the first Hopeman Town, this play would have been twice the length.'

Nimrod furrowed his brow. 'I don't know what you mean.'

'The original town of Little Creek is over there.' Haywood gestured towards the window. 'When the railroad arrived they moved down the tracks and started again. I can't have my characters say they want to build a town nearby. It sounds better if they say they'll build a town on this very spot.'

Nimrod thought for a moment and then smiled.

'I reckon I'm starting to understand.'

Haywood pushed the sheaf across the table and sat back in his chair.

'Take *Hopeman's Legacy* away and read it. Then you'll see what I've done – but take care. I have only two copies.'

'I'll do that.' Nimrod reckoned that after he'd read the play he'd get more opportunities to probe Haywood about the other truths he'd left out, and all without making him suspicious, but he couldn't resist asking one last question: 'What's the biggest fact you've ignored because it's too messy?'

'That was an easy one to ignore because everyone else ignores it.' Haywood glanced at the bar where Jessica and Wallace were still talking. 'Leopold Hopeman was murdered.'

CHAPTER 6

'So you've decided to visit the old town,' Sydney said when Nimrod found him in the Hard Trails saloon the next morning.

'I thought it was worth the risk,' Nimrod said. 'But we shouldn't be seen talking together, so we need to be quick.'

'The people here have their own problems, so they won't be interested in us.'

Sydney called to Oliver Peak, the saloon owner, to bring them drinks, but Nimrod shook his head.

'I need to show you something.'

With that, they headed outside. They walked past the few buildings that stood beside the tracks and which comprised the remnants of the old town until they reached the location Haywood had told Nimrod about. As it turned out, there was nothing to see other than patches of darker ground that marked

59

where buildings had once stood.

'What did you want to show me?' Sydney asked with a frown when they stopped beside the tracks.

'This is the original town,' Nimrod said. 'They abandoned it and started up again beyond the depot.'

'I already know that.'

'And this is the spot where Leopold Hopeman was murdered.'

'I didn't know that.' Sydney tipped back his hat to scratch his forehead. 'I've talked to dozens of people and nobody mentioned that.'

Nimrod nodded. 'It seems nobody talks about it. Even Haywood Milton, whose play relates the story of this town, sees no reason to include it.'

'Who killed him?'

'His name was Ezra Howe. He robbed Leopold, but Leopold fought back. Ezra shot him and ran, but he was killed in Black Creek.'

Sydney shrugged. 'It sounds like an unfortunate incident rather than something sinister.'

'Maybe it was, but just before he was killed Leopold wrote a will leaving all his money to the townsfolk.' Nimrod looked at Sydney until with a wince he conceded that the timing was suspicious. 'In addition, the lawman who killed Ezra was Marshal Farr.'

'That man catching an outlaw could be the oddest

thing of all. I'll see if anyone knows anything about Ezra.' Sydney glanced down the tracks towards the main town. 'The only development I have to report is that the old town's days are numbered. With the main town expanding it needs more space and it'll soon overcome the remaining buildings.'

'If the town absorbs both areas, it might improve things.'

'Nobody here thinks so. But Trinity doesn't like it that these old buildings are the first ones newcomers see. He plans to demolish them and rebuild. As the fund owns most of them, he can do whatever he likes.'

Nimrod shrugged. 'I'm not sure that's connected to our investigation other than it's another reminder of the past that's about to be destroyed.'

Sydney nodded and moved to head back to the saloon, but then stopped and glanced back at Nimrod.

'Be careful,' he said. 'Someone's watching us from beside the nearest depot warehouse.'

Nimrod acknowledged the warning with a nod. Then, while Sydney headed away, he mooched around the area. He found nothing of interest beyond noting that as the buildings had been close together, either Leopold had just been unlucky that the killer had robbed his house, or he had been targeted deliberately.

When he'd finished he headed back towards town with his head down as if in thought, although he kept his eyes raised – and that let him see the watcher who had worried Sydney. The man was walking away, and the moment he moved out of view Nimrod broke into a run.

When he reached the warehouse the man had already moved past the depot, having presumably started running at the same time as he had. The man was too far away for Nimrod to see him clearly and he soon scooted into hiding between two buildings.

Nimrod slowed down and walked into town, reckoning that continuing his pursuit would only alert anyone else who might be watching him to the fact that he knew he was being watched. He had agreed to report to the theatre at noon for a rehearsal of Haywood's play, and when he arrived he stopped to read the playbill on the door detailing the first performance of *Hopeman's Legacy*.

He was rewarded for his caution when, reflected in a window, he saw a man looking his way from the side of a hotel. He was the right build to be the man who had watched him from the depot, but the reflection wasn't clear enough to let him see his features.

He resisted the urge to turn around to get a better look, and headed inside to find that Haywood and his actors had already gathered. Lawrence Saunders was sitting in the front row, giving him his first look at the man Trinity had hired him to investigate.

'Where do you want me to lie?' Nimrod said when he joined Haywood on the stage. 'The play didn't describe where I'll be.'

'Over there,' Haywood said gesturing at the middle of the stage. 'Don't move and don't trip anyone up.'

Nimrod headed to the indicated area where he adopted a dramatic pose lying on his back with a hand clutched to his chest. Haywood shook his head and told him to lie on his front with his head cradled in his arms.

Then the rehearsal got underway with the opening scene in which his body was discovered. Nimrod listened, although he found that remaining still was harder than he had expected, and it took him most of the next hour to work out how to relax on the hard floor.

The play had two acts, and the first ended on a dramatic note in which Trinity and Alexander confronted each other with their different plans for the legacy.

Haywood called for a break and gathered the actors around him to deliver his criticisms. As he reckoned his performance had been beyond reproach, after he'd freed the cramps from his limbs, Nimrod took the opportunity to sit with Lawrence.

'You were a convincing dead man,' Lawrence said.

'I gave my all in my performance,' Nimrod said.

Lawrence smiled. 'I'd guess as a detective you've had plenty of experience of death.'

'I have, and that's why I'm enjoying spending time away from investigating.'

Nimrod reckoned Lawrence must have had an ulterior motive in mentioning his line of work, and the flicker in Lawrence's eyes suggested he had noted Nimrod's attempt to allay his fears.

Lawrence then moved on to speak with Haywood. He provided some back-slapping praise before picking another seat away from him.

Nimrod didn't mind that Lawrence suspected he was investigating him, as that might make him behave differently, but before he could work out what his next move should be, Haywood joined him.

'Do you now see why I told you to lie comfortably rather than dramatically?' he said.

'I do, although I had thought you didn't want me to look as if I'd been shot, bearing in mind that nobody mentions how I died.'

Haywood shook his head. 'As I told you, that's a messy detail, and as you've now read the play I assume you can see that I've concocted a fascinating tale from often confusing events.'

Nimrod shrugged. 'I do, although some of the things you've done surprised me, such as your portrayal of Alexander. I've met him, and I didn't enjoy the experience. Yet in the play he's a reasonable man who just has a different opinion to Trinity.'

'I've heard Alexander's side of the story and it differed to everyone else's, so I compromised.' Haywood smiled. 'And I promised him I'd depict him as a successful businessman.'

Nimrod snorted a laugh. 'Which means that what you've written won't annoy him.'

Haywood winked, as if his reasoning should have been obvious.

'Of course.'

Nimrod rubbed his jaw as he considered whether to continue complaining when he was unlikely to get an answer he liked, and then pressed on anyhow.

'I accept that, but you've still put in the arguments that took place, except Clayton is the aggressor, and he's the one person who can't complain about the way he's been depicted.'

'Drama requires a villain, and as his wife hasn't objected I must have distilled the essence of the truth.'

'You may have presented an acceptable version of events, but you must be worried that anyone who sees your play will assume it's more valid than the truth.'

Haywood shrugged and then beckoned for his actors to gather together for the second act.

'That is not for me to worry about,' he said.

'Perhaps it isn't,' Nimrod said as he stood up, 'but

maybe others will welcome the truth being buried by your fiction.'

Haywood paused, Nimrod's jibe appearing to have concerned him, before he dismissed the matter with a clap of the hands. Nimrod then resumed his place on stage, but as it turned out the second act didn't run smoothly.

The earlier rehearsals had concentrated on the first act, so the second act stuttered with awkward pauses and scenes having to be restarted. Whenever someone made a mistake, Haywood barked out complaints in an irritated manner that caused tempers to fray.

Later Nimrod laid a spare jacket on the floor and headed to a seat. Nobody objected, but he found that Lawrence had also become bored with proceedings and had left.

The afternoon dragged on. Nimrod stayed in the hope of getting another chance to talk with Lawrence, but he didn't return. As it became clear that this rehearsal would meander on into the evening he made his excuses, without being acknowledged, and went in search of Jessica, as she had been eager to give him more information about Leopold.

He didn't look out for his watcher as he didn't expect him to have had the patience to wait outside the theatre for a large part of the day. But when he reached the first saloon, from the corner of his eye he noticed someone on the other side of the main drag keeping pace with him.

He ignored him and slipped into the saloon to find that Jessica wasn't there, but Wallace was at the bar. He saw no reason to speak with him, so he started to turn away. Then he saw Hubert Latham, which made him stop as he had a new thought about his mysterious watcher. He headed to the bar.

'Are you being sensible and avoiding Buck Garrett?' Hubert said when Nimrod stood beside him.

'I am, but I'm still confused about what happened that night.' Nimrod leaned towards him. 'When you found me and Buck you reckoned you'd seen another man.'

Nimrod gestured for the bartender to give Hubert a drink.

'I did, but I haven't thought about it since.' Hubert glanced aside as he appeared to think back.

'So Marshal Farr hasn't questioned you yet?'

Hubert gave a bemused shrug. 'He hasn't. Then again I didn't see much. A man was watching the alley before the shooting. I thought I saw him again later, but he left before you and Buck met up.'

'I assume you haven't seen this man again.'

'I haven't.' Hubert narrowed his eyes. 'Although I'm guessing you have.'

'Someone's following me.' Nimrod frowned. 'It

could be the same man, so it might be best if you don't tell anyone what you saw.'

'I sure won't,' Hubert said.

Then with a shiver as if he'd just worked out that this meant that even speaking with Nimrod was risky, Hubert picked up his glass and without looking at Nimrod again, left the bar.

'What did he see?' Wallace asked from further down the bar. He was twenty feet away and looking straight ahead, but clearly he had overheard some of their conversation.

'That's not important,' Nimrod said when he joined him.

'I'm sure anything that man says is of no interest to me, but I hope you're different. So is Lawrence Saunders cheating us?'

'My last mission failed because Alexander Caldwell revealed my identity with idle chatter. I can see you have something in common with him.'

'I have nothing in common with Alexander other than a hatred of people who try to take advantage of me. So I ask again: is he cheating us?'

Wallace had lowered his voice when he'd repeated his question, so Nimrod smiled as he leaned closer.

'He already suspects I took a role in Haywood's play so I could spy on him. That's either because someone told him about my mission or because he has a guilty conscience.'

'Then it must be the latter.' Wallace turned to him. 'When can we confront him with the truth?'

'I've yet to get any proof, but I've spent only a short while with him, and complex operations take time.'

'Understood. You have until Saturday to expose him, because then I might not have to sit through Haywood's damn play.'

Nimrod gave a supportive smile, but Wallace didn't return it, suggesting he hadn't been joking.

'I'll do my best.' He looked around. 'Where's Jessica?'

'Jessica can be found only when she wants to be found. If you want to speak with her, I suggest you stop looking.'

Wallace gave him a long look that implied there was more wisdom in his comment than Nimrod had detected. Nimrod nodded and left the saloon.

He turned towards the next saloon while casually looking for his watcher, but then decided that Wallace's cryptic statement meant Jessica wasn't in any of her usual places. So he decided not to question her that night and headed back to his hotel and then up to his room – but he stopped in the corridor when he saw that his door was open.

Although he assumed Sydney was waiting for him, he moved quietly to the side of the door and peered inside. To his surprise Jessica was sitting beside the bed leafing through a journal.

'You're late,' she said with a terse tone.

'And you're in my room,' he said, moving inside.

'As you're in my hotel I could argue with that, but I thought it was important you read this.' She held up the journal and then softened her tone and her expression. 'It's my late husband's and there's one section that'll interest you.'

'Which one?' he asked.

She slammed the book shut and tossed it on to the bed.

'I could show you now, or I could show you later,' she said with a playful smile and with her gaze still set on the bed.

'Later will do,' Nimrod said, closing the door behind him.

CHAPTER 7

It was the morning when Nimrod got to read the relevant part of Clayton's journal, and at first he didn't think it was as important as Jessica had thought it was. The entry complained that the good mood Leopold Hopeman's legacy had fostered had now been eroded. Clayton wrote about his loathing of the changes to the town, with new people arriving in the hope of gaining something by being close to the lucky beneficiaries.

Nimrod became more interested in Clayton's complaints when he wrote about one man who concerned him. This man loitered around the saloon and rarely talked, but his constant watching made people nervous. With his intrigue growing, Nimrod turned over the page only to find there was nothing more. As Clayton wrote most weeks and the book was only a quarter full, he must have died shortly after making his last entry.

Nimrod had promised to return the book to Jessica, but now that he knew there wasn't much to read, he worked his way through the rest of the journal. It started a month after Leopold's death, and the comments were the same as the later entry, bemoaning the recent changes.

Nimrod found them interesting mainly because of what they didn't say. Clayton had no problem with Trinity, Wallace or Alexander, and he had nothing but praise for his wife. In support of Sydney's theory, he didn't come across as a man who was seething with rage and who would die during an argument with Alexander. Instead he was someone who had enjoyed the quiet life more than the life the legacy was bringing them.

Nimrod was coming to the end of his reading when one comment took him aback. Clayton talked about his dislike for another newcomer to town, Lawrence Saunders, who was trying to ingratiate himself with everyone, a type of behaviour that suggested he was a disreputable fellow. This was the only mention of him, however, and shortly afterwards he reached the final entry, which he read again before returning the journal to Jessica in her room.

'Are you pleased you persuaded me to give you the journal?' she said, peering at him around the door.

'You certainly took some convincing,' Nimrod said

with a wink. 'But I'm more interested in knowing why you wanted me to know your husband was worried about Lawrence and a mysterious newcomer.'

'You're the detective. Figure it out.' She started to close the door, but then stopped. 'If you don't, you know where my room is.'

Nimrod smiled, and then moved on to seek out Sydney. The previous day he hadn't told him about the depiction of his father in Haywood's play, as he feared he would react badly, but now that he'd read Clayton's private thoughts he reckoned he could provide a more balanced opinion on Clayton. Even so, he resolved not to mention his dalliance with Jessica. But as it turned out, when he reached the old part of town he couldn't give Sydney an update.

Sydney was standing outside the Hard Trails saloon with Oliver Peak, who was giving orders to around twenty men. Then some of the men hurried away to stand beside the buildings, while others formed two lines directed towards the depot.

'What's happening?' Nimrod asked when he had worked his way through the throng.

'The battle for the old town is about to begin,' Sydney said, and then pointed, indicating Mayor Tucker and Buck, who were walking past the depot. 'Trinity's coming to issue his ultimatum, so we're providing a show of strength.'

The sight made the rest of Oliver's men troop

inside and stand at the windows, while Oliver stood in the saloon doorway.

'And who will hear that ultimatum?' Nimrod said.

Sydney didn't answer, and when Oliver smiled at him Nimrod figured he could answer his own question. Sydney then slipped into the saloon to avoid drawing attention to himself, so Nimrod moved away.

When Trinity and Buck started walking between the two lines of men, Nimrod hailed Trinity with a raised hand.

'I'm surprised you've been chosen to speak for the old town,' Trinity said when he joined Nimrod.

'I wasn't chosen,' Nimrod said. 'I just happened to be here.'

'Which still begs the question: why are you here?'

'I'm doing my job.' Nimrod spread his hands. 'When I've heard you out, I'll tell Oliver. Then I'll get back to doing it.'

Trinity looked him over with narrowed eyes, as he clearly wondered whether he was being deceived; he then returned to his usual affable demeanour.

'Then tell him this: at sundown these buildings will be demolished so suitable buildings can be erected.'

'When can everyone move back into these suitable buildings?'

'They won't, and I don't care where they go,' Trinity said with studied finality. 'Soon, instead of this squalor the first thing anyone arriving on the train will see is a thriving part of town.'

Nimrod shrugged. 'This area is no worse than most of Black Creek, but I'm surprised you want to destroy the past, bearing in mind it all started in the Hard Trails saloon.'

Trinity cast the saloon a disdainful look.

'Men who look back never move forwards. Now talk to Oliver. Then on the way back you can brief me on your investigation.'

'I welcome the opportunity,' Nimrod said.

The stern expressions sported by the men glaring out of the windows suggested that nobody would welcome Trinity's message. Sure enough, as Nimrod headed towards the saloon, the men on either side of Trinity closed ranks.

Trinity noted their ominous behaviour and moved nearer to Buck, who rested a hand on his holster. If he had hoped that despite being outnumbered Buck's reputation would quell the discontent, he'd have been disappointed, as everyone edged closer.

When Nimrod reached the doorway, Oliver didn't even meet his eye, suggesting he had gathered the essence of Trinity's statement. Then Oliver raised a hand, making his men surround Trinity and Buck.

Most of the men were armed, but they kept their guns holstered. To his credit Trinity placed a hand on Buck's shoulder, making him move his hand away from his holster.

Buck was disarmed, and he and Trinity were bundled along. When they reached the saloon, Trinity faced Oliver.

'Assaulting your mayor was a bad mistake,' he said. 'It changes nothing.'

'I don't reckon so,' Oliver said. 'I know how this town works.'

'The town must become respectable. This is the only way.'

'Find another way. You have until sundown.' Oliver gestured and Trinity was moved into the saloon, but Buck was kept outside so he could address him. 'Fetch Jessica and Wallace. They'll need to support Trinity's decision to leave us alone.'

The men holding Buck released him, but Buck didn't move.

'I follow only Trinity's orders,' he said.

'He'll be safe until sundown, but if you want this to get ugly earlier than that, stay here.'

For long moments Buck glared at Oliver.

'If any harm comes to him, I'll do it back to you ten times over.' Then with a roll of his shoulders, Buck turned away. He barged the men who had accosted him aside and headed back towards the main town.

Oliver then ordered the men left outside to take up lookout positions around the saloon, his instructions ending when he faced Nimrod.

'You're Sydney's friend, so you can join him,' he said.

'I reckon I should follow Buck,' Nimrod said.

'You suspect treachery?'

'I suspect you won't get what you want without a fight.'

Oliver nodded and beckoned for Nimrod to leave. So Nimrod hurried after Buck, who had now reached the first warehouse.

Buck was looking straight ahead, so Nimrod hurried up. He had got to within fifty paces of him when Buck reached the town. He had expected that Buck would go to one of Jessica's saloons or hotels, but instead he headed to the theatre. At the door he stopped to glance around – at the time several people were around Nimrod, so Buck didn't show any sign of having noticed him before he went inside.

Nimrod broke into a run and reached the door thirty seconds later, but when he heard approaching footfalls, he jerked backwards. He backtracked and had reached the corner of the theatre when a man emerged.

The man was looking into the theatre, giving Nimrod enough time to lean against the wall and look elsewhere. Nimrod waited for a few moments and then glanced at the man, finding that he was now walking across the main drag and looking straight ahead.

Nimrod hadn't seen his watcher from close to before, but he had the same build and walked with the same easy motion as this man. Enough of his face was visible for Nimrod to see that his features weren't memorable, suggesting a reason why he had been able to watch him secretly.

He reckoned Buck must have met him, a possibility that became more likely when Buck stepped into the doorway and was evidently watching the man. When the man disappeared from view, Buck advanced on Nimrod.

'Who is he?' Nimrod asked, standing his ground.

'You're the detective,' Buck said. 'Figure it out.'

'You're the second person to say that to me today.'

'Then it's good advice.'

Buck reached him and shoved his shoulder, making him step backwards. Nimrod bristled, but then saw that Buck was looking at the alley beside the theatre, so he turned away.

When they were in the alley where they couldn't be heard by passers-by, Nimrod gestured in the direction the watcher had gone, and said:

'Oliver told you to fetch Jessica and Wallace, except you met a man who lurks in the shadows. That suggests you expect a violent end to the showdown in the Hard Trails saloon.'

'That end is obvious to anyone. Then again, I'd

78

heard you were a terrible Pinkerton detective.'

Nimrod frowned. 'How would you know about my time as a Pinkerton?'

Buck chuckled and leaned forwards to whisper in his ear.

'Because unlike you, I'm still one,' he said.

CHAPTER 8

'You're no detective,' Nimrod said. 'You're just Trinity's brutal bodyguard.'

'Believe what you will,' Buck said, leaning back from him. 'All I want from you is that you keep my secret and you don't interfere with my investigation.'

'What investigation?'

Buck sneered. 'I'm not revealing that to a man who on his last mission had his cover exposed due to incompetence.'

'That wasn't my fault, but I still. . . .' Nimrod cringed back a step when Buck rounded on him.

'You're not listening. I told you what I'm doing because I need you to stay out of my way. Do that, or I'll deal with you.'

Buck raised an arm to shove Nimrod's shoulder again, but this time Nimrod grabbed Buck's wrist before he could touch him.

'I'm investigating the Excelsior theatre, a place

where you met that man. So stay out of my way or I'll deal with *you*.'

Buck glanced at Nimrod's hand and shook his head.

'I know about all of your investigations. So let's hope that nothing bad happens to the people from the old town today.'

Nimrod couldn't tell whether Buck was revealing he knew about Sydney, but he figured that anything he said could make it clear he'd had dealings with him, so without comment he opened his hand and stepped away. Buck looked him over and snarled before he left the alley.

Buck headed into the Long Night saloon, so Nimrod stood at the front of the theatre. Presently Buck and Wallace emerged, and walked to the hotel where Nimrod was staying. For the next ten minutes several men went into and then left the hotel. They were all armed, and they all headed towards the old town.

Then Buck came outside with Jessica and Wallace. Buck gestured, seemingly to people positioned around town, making Nimrod conclude he had organized something. He had enough time to get ahead of the group and report to Oliver, but he reckoned he might achieve more by taking a risk. He set off for the hotel and when Jessica saw him coming she beckoned him on.

'I gather you know about our problem,' she said breezily when he arrived. 'I reckon Buck would welcome your help.'

When Buck firmed his jaw Nimrod couldn't avoid smiling.

'I'm sure Buck has the situation under control,' he said. 'I've come to make sure you're safe.'

Buck took a deep intake of breath and Wallace muttered to himself, but Jessica appeared to revel in their disapproval as, with a smile, she looped her arm in his before they moved on.

'I already feel safe,' she said.

'And I'm already pleased that this situation has let me spend more time with you.'

Wallace cast an exasperated glance at Buck, but Buck ignored him. Then they walked on through the town. Several people stopped them to talk. Buck spoke to each person quietly, after which they hurried away. From the scraps of conversation Nimrod overheard he gathered that these people had heard there was trouble, and Buck was confirming it.

As he reckoned Buck had already organized gunmen to go to the Hard Trails saloon, he didn't know why he was informing yet more people. Despite the distractions, Buck ensured they maintained a steady pace until they reached the depot.

'Stay back and I'll do the talking,' he said. Then he

strode on ahead, so they were a dozen yards behind him when the saloon first came into view.

'I hope he can sort this out without trouble,' Jessica said to Wallace with a low voice that was different to her usual light way of speaking.

'We have no choice but to trust him, again,' Wallace said as, like Jessica, he spoke using a level tone instead of his usual snide approach.

'He works for Trinity,' Nimrod said. 'He'll make sure no harm comes to him.'

'When men like him are involved, someone always suffers,' Wallace said. 'That's why Jessica is holding your arm tightly.'

Jessica patted Nimrod's arm. Then, as Buck stopped beside the last warehouse, they all halted to await developments. Several minutes passed before Oliver emerged from the saloon with two gunmen flanking him.

Oliver beckoned for Buck and the others to approach, but Buck set his feet wide apart in a show of his not moving. From a hundred yards apart the two men glared at each other until, with a nod to the gunmen on each side, Oliver moved on.

He stopped at the mid-point between the warehouse and the saloon, where he set his feet wide apart in an apparent mimicry of Buck's posture. Buck snorted and walked towards Oliver, stopping twenty paces away from him.

'I've done what you asked,' he called. 'Jessica and Wallace are here. Bring Trinity out and we can talk.'

'Trinity goes nowhere until everyone agrees to my terms,' Oliver said.

'Jessica and Wallace have come only because they don't want this to become a bloodbath, but they accept it can end in only two ways: either you give up, or you're made to give up.'

Oliver shrugged. 'It's not yet noon, so there's plenty of time before sundown for them to agree to a third outcome.'

'You haven't got until sundown. You have until noon. Then it'll end for all of you, although I'll make sure you stay alive for long enough to regret defying your mayor.'

'As long as you do nothing foolish, Trinity is safe.' Oliver spread his hands. 'So do we start this, or are you going to make more hollow threats?'

When Buck folded his arms, beside the warehouse Jessica directed an alarmed look at Wallace.

'Do something,' she whispered. 'This is going to turn bad very soon.'

'What can I do?' Wallace said. 'I can't talk Oliver down.'

'Someone has to. The gunmen will already be here, and the townsfolk won't be far behind.'

Jessica and Wallace faced each other. With them again speaking in what sounded like an honest manner despite his presence, Nimrod reckoned he might have learned something that helped Sydney's mission. This was that Wallace was a weak man who lived off the hard work of others, while Jessica cared about people. These traits suggested they hadn't killed Clayton, which meant Sydney's suspicions could be valid, and the confrontational Mayor Tucker was more likely to be responsible.

'Then I'll do it,' Nimrod said, and when that made Jessica smile he disentangled his arm from hers. 'Stay here, and stay out of any trouble that erupts.'

'I sure will,' Wallace said, his comment making Jessica laugh before she brushed a kiss against Nimrod's cheek.

Then Nimrod moved on, his intervention making Oliver look past Buck to watch him approach.

'Buck's threats aren't hollow,' Nimrod said when he was standing beside Buck. 'It's almost noon, so be sensible and do a deal.'

Buck grunted in approval of Nimrod's statement, but Oliver shook his head.

'No deal,' Oliver said. 'I've seen Buck's gunmen moving closer, but he's bluffing. Trinity won't let Buck quell a disturbance by shooting the townsfolk. It'll be bad for business.'

Oliver's faith in his plan impressed Nimrod, but as he could see no way to dent his commitment he looked around for proof that this situation was about to go wrong for him.

Several gunmen were moving beyond the rail tracks on a circuitous route to the saloon, while other men were walking beside the warehouses. He had expected this, but he also saw movement in town, and in a shocking moment he understood Buck's plan.

'Let me talk to Trinity,' he said. 'He'll listen to me.'

Oliver furrowed his brow, but then beckoned for Nimrod to join him in retreating to the saloon.

'What will you say to make him give in?' Oliver said when they'd moved out of Buck's hearing.

'That I know Buck's plan.'

Oliver frowned, but he said no more until they reached the saloon where he ordered the two gunmen to keep watch outside. When he headed inside, Trinity was sitting at a table with a man standing guard over him.

Sydney was beside a window watching the depot, although he nodded to Nimrod.

'Nimrod has a proposition for you, Trinity,' Oliver called.

Oliver had stopped beside the door, so as it would look odd if Nimrod tried to have a quiet word with Trinity, he spoke loudly ensuring everyone heard him.

'Buck has plenty of guns aimed at the saloon, but he won't use them,' he said. 'Like Oliver, he knows that impoverished townsfolk getting shot won't look good for this town.'

'And I know that the mayor getting harmed won't help Oliver,' Trinity said, turning to him. 'So what's the proposition?'

'Wallace and Jessica don't have the stomach for this, but in a few minutes they'll have to watch events unfold. You can stop those events.'

'But you just said Buck won't use his gunmen.'

'They're not here to storm the saloon. They're here as back-up.' Nimrod put a hand to his ear even though he had yet to hear anything. 'A mob of enraged townsfolk is coming to free you. Any casualties will be viewed as a just consequence when a town that's proud of itself shows its displeasure.'

Trinity shrugged, not reacting with alarm as Nimrod had hoped, but his statement made Oliver hurry to the window where Sydney was keeping watch. Sydney moved from side to side before pointing.

'You're right,' Oliver said before he turned to Nimrod. 'A lot of people are heading this way. How can we stop this?'

'You can't. Wallace and Jessica are decent folk and they don't want anyone to die. Only Trinity can do anything.'

Nimrod's comment made Sydney look at him, confirming he'd picked up on the implication behind his statement that as Trinity was different to Jessica and Wallace, he could have killed Clayton.

'I support my townsfolk,' Trinity said, folding his arms. 'They won't want their mayor to give in to threats.'

As Oliver and Trinity looked at each other, for the first time Nimrod heard the approaching people. Men were chanting, making everyone in the saloon glance nervously at each other, but Oliver smiled.

'It'd seem we'll have a bigger audience than I'd intended.' Oliver clapped his hands as he tried to bolster his men's courage. 'Keep Trinity secure while I show everyone the truth about this town.'

Oliver glared at Trinity, seemingly hoping his confidence might make him back down, but Trinity turned away. Oliver sighed and stood beside the door.

With the men who weren't guarding Trinity settling down beside the windows as they waited for the townsfolk to arrive, Nimrod headed across the saloon towards Sydney – but then he smelt something that made him stop. He sniffed, and that made him cough before he turned to Oliver.

'I smell burning,' he said. 'There's a fire somewhere.'

Supporting his belief, Sydney coughed and looked to the back of the saloon.

A moment later a puff of smoke burst through the wall and spread out as it rose up. Then the shooting started outside.

CHAPTER 9

'Someone in the mob shot at us, but who's trying to smoke us out?' Oliver shouted.

'Buck's gunmen and the townsfolk are too far away,' Nimrod said, 'but who did it isn't as important as putting the fire out.'

As Nimrod didn't want to annoy Trinity by helping Oliver to defend the saloon, he indicated he'd check it out. When Oliver didn't object he ran to the door. He slipped outside, and with his back to the wall, hurried to the corner of the building. He peered down the side of the saloon, and ascertained that the situation wasn't as bad as he'd feared.

Flames were licking at the wall of the derelict stable that stood next to the saloon, and burning planks had fallen away to lie against the saloon wall. As this was unlikely to be an accident, he moved on cautiously. When he reached the nearest planks he kicked them away from the saloon, finding to his relief that even though they had made smoke pour inside, the flames had yet to burn the wall.

He removed more planks, and reckoned he was making the saloon safe when a gunshot rattled. The blast echoed between the buildings and it made Nimrod duck down and look for the shooter. More gunfire erupted, but this time it came from the saloon as Oliver's men responded. Heartened by the possibility that the shot hadn't been aimed at him, Nimrod straightened up again.

He resumed kicking away planks, but then another shot blasted nearby. This time a flurry of gunsmoke emerged from a gap between two planks in the stable wall, while splinters kicked away from the saloon wall confirmed that he had been the target.

Nimrod aimed his gun at the stable, but he couldn't see the shooter. So in a sudden decision he leapt over the burning planks.

He was in mid-air when to his horror he saw that he'd misjudged how many planks he had to clear. Then he crashed down amidst the burning debris, but his momentum kept him moving and with a tumbling roll he came clear of the fire.

He rolled twice more and batted burning embers from his clothes. Then he looked back, finding that his ungainly passage through the fire had knocked most of the burning debris away from the saloon and had opened up a gap that would let him get into the stable.

The fire had yet to take hold of the stable, so he hurried on. With his head down he burst into the building and then slid to a halt facing the length of wall where the shooter had been. Nobody was there, so he swirled round. The interior was an open space with nowhere to take cover, but he still couldn't locate the shooter.

'Don't move,' someone said in the shadows at the far corner of the stable. Nimrod didn't recognize the voice.

'Your plan to torch the saloon has failed,' Nimrod said.

The man snorted. 'You don't know what my plan is.'

Nimrod nodded, as the man's choice of words probably identified him.

'As you have a plan, you're not just following Buck's orders.' Nimrod turned towards the corner, although he still couldn't see the man. 'Why have you been watching me?'

The man laughed. 'As I reckon you've already been told: you're the detective, so figure it out.'

Raised voices and angry demands were coming from near the saloon as the mob approached so, as he hadn't been warned for moving, Nimrod looked along both walls. This time he saw a gap in the back wall.

With a grunt of irritation he ran across the stable and looked through the gap. A man was fleeing, and although he then moved behind the next building, the fleeting glimpse that Nimrod had of him confirmed he had spoken with his watcher.

He considered giving chase, but as the noise made by the townsfolk was growing louder he headed to the alley, finding that the fire had almost burnt itself out. He moved on to the front of the saloon where around seventy people were storming closer.

Buck and his gunmen were watching the scene, while a handful of Oliver's men stood before the doorway with guns brandished. These men had worried expressions, confirming that they didn't want to shoot into the crowd.

Nimrod checked that Wallace and Jessica were staying away from the trouble and then moved on to the door, reaching it at the same time as the mob met up with Oliver's men. The townsfolk were greeted with defiant threats, and two men fired into the air, but then they were swept along without slowing down the advancing throng.

With dismay Nimrod turned his back on the fist-shaking men and slipped into the saloon. Inside Oliver was striding back and forth, checking out the scene through the windows while his men looked at him for guidance.

'The fire's out, but you're about to lose the

saloon,' Nimrod called to him. 'Do a deal with Trinity before it's too late.'

Oliver shook his head a moment before the saloon doors burst open and the mob charged in. The men were being pushed from behind, and the first wave went sprawling on to the floor, making the next wave stumble when they couldn't find a place to stand.

With their arrival being so disorganized, Oliver had enough time to bark out instructions for his men to stand before the bar and face the onslaught. The man guarding Trinity dragged him to his feet, but then Sydney joined them and spoke with the guard.

When that man nodded, Sydney wrapped an arm around Trinity's neck from behind while jabbing his gun into his side. Trinity tensed, but he still showed no sign of backing down.

'No further!' Oliver shouted, facing the newcomers.

His demand slowed down the slew of people trying to get inside, although that let the men who had fallen over stand up and stop blocking the entrance. Oliver shouted his demand again, and this time the people spilling inside stopped, although they still outnumbered Oliver's men by three to one.

The two sides faced each other. Then several people near to the doorway parted to reveal they had captured two of Oliver's men. Both men had battered faces and they were unconscious. With contempt they were thrown to the floor in the space between the opposing sides.

'You're all next,' someone shouted from the group, making a cheer go up.

Oliver shouted a warning, but his words were drowned out, as with yells of defiance the mob surged forwards. Someone fired a gun, and that led to a burst of gunfire, but then Nimrod was surrounded by shouting men.

He slugged the jaw of the first man to reach him, knocking him into the people behind him, and punched the next man in the stomach. Then everyone's forward motion pushed him backwards, and he was carried along until he crunched into the bar.

At least three men held him, ensuring he couldn't move to either side, so Nimrod let the pressure of the numerous bodies bend him over the bar. Then he twisted and scrambled until he squeezed out from the block of men so he could lie on the bar.

He got to his knees and looked over the crowd, seeing yet more men pour into the saloon. He couldn't see Oliver's men, but the gaps in the sea of writhing figures showed him where scuffles were on-going.

Nimrod stood up to get a better idea about what was happening, but that drew attention to him. Someone grabbed his leg and pulled. He kicked out, knocking his opponent away, only for two more men to take his place and gather a firmer hold of his ankles and knees. They tugged, crashing him down on to his side before they dragged him forward.

As he feared for his life if he were to be pulled back into the mob, Nimrod flailed his arms and kicked his opponents. The blows loosened the hands that clamped around his legs, and as so many men were reaching for him that they were getting in each other's way, he dragged himself clear.

He rolled backwards over a shoulder and dropped down on the other side of the bar. Then he bounded back up and looked to either side for a way out. But with people flanking both ends of the bar, he had trapped himself. Then he noticed that the only other people who had headed behind the bar were Sydney and Trinity.

Sydney held a gun on the mayor, but Trinity had a confident smile. Moving slowly, Sydney raised the gun to press it into Trinity's neck, ensuring that the nearest men saw him.

Within moments, space opened up around their end of the bar. As Sydney now knew that Trinity had probably killed his father, Nimrod set off towards them. He tried to catch Sydney's eye, but someone reached over the bar and grabbed his shoulders. He jerked away from his assailant, but the man had gathered a strong grip and pulled him back. Worse, cold metal was pressed up against his neck in the same way that Trinity was threatened.

'Release the mayor,' his captor shouted. 'Oliver's dead, and the rest will die if you harm him.'

Sydney sneered, suggesting that as long as he could kill Trinity he didn't care about anyone else's fate. Even when he looked at the gunman holding Nimrod his expression didn't change.

Trinity must have gathered that Sydney was resolute, as he fidgeted, forcing Sydney to drag him closer, which made the nearest men edge forwards. Then Sydney leaned over Trinity's shoulder and whispered in his ear.

Nimrod couldn't hear what he said, but it made Trinity flinch so strongly it almost dislodged Sydney's tight grip of him. Then he stood rigidly and raised a shaking hand, his action silencing the hubbub in the saloon.

'I thank you all for your support, but no more of our townsfolk will be harmed today,' he said, his low voice being different to his usual confident way of speaking.

'We're not threatening nobody,' someone said.

'Yeah,' another man said. 'You're the one being threatened by these no-good varmints.'

Trinity cast a sideways glance at Sydney, and then the two men locked gazes. A silent message must have passed between them, as Sydney lowered his gun, letting Trinity step aside. A few moments later Nimrod was released.

'I am no longer under threat,' Trinity said. He straightened his jacket and hat as he regained his composure. When he spoke again he used his usual affable way of speaking. 'I'm proud of the way you all banded together, but I'm sorry I failed you.'

'You sure didn't fail nobody,' someone shouted, his comment receiving a round of supportive mutterings that grew in volume, even when Trinity waved his arms calling for quiet.

'You're wrong,' he called, speaking over everyone and making the comments cease. 'I take full responsibility for this incident, and now I'll respond appropriately by promising to preserve the old part of town and making sure that a situation like this never happens again.'

A few half-hearted supportive comments sounded, but with the stand-off over, people at the back of the crowd slipped outside while others turned away. When Trinity moved out from behind the bar and began shaking hands with his rescuers, Sydney joined Nimrod.

'He sure changed his mind quickly,' Nimrod said. 'What did you say to him?'

'I reckon you can guess that,' Sydney said. 'I told him I'm Clayton's son.'

CHAPTER 10

Two people had died in the fight to free Mayor Tucker. Oliver had been shot, while the other man had been trampled to death during the saloon invasion. This man was a member of the mob, and as there were numerous other minor injuries on both sides, the fact that there were equal losses to each side appeared to subdue everyone's spirits.

Within ten minutes of Trinity declaring the situation over, the crowd had dispersed. Trinity left the saloon with the stragglers and without speaking to Sydney again, while Buck and his gunmen didn't even approach the saloon.

'So what happens now?' Nimrod asked Sydney when the remaining men set about righting tables and trying to make sense of the recent events.

'I hope that now you've joined me in suspecting that Trinity killed my father you can find proof, but as regards what the old town does now, I don't know.'

'Trinity sounded like he'd relented.'

'Trinity sounded like a politician. He said what he

had to say so he got to walk away, but I wouldn't trust him to help anyone here, especially as Oliver died.'

Nimrod agreed with that, so they stood in silence until someone pointed out that Marshal Farr was heading towards the saloon.

'I'll explain what happened here,' Nimrod said. 'Although I doubt he'll do anything about it.'

Sydney shook his head. 'I'll talk to him. Now that I've spoken with Trinity, I'm not keeping my head down any longer.'

'I'll leave you, then.' Nimrod noted the time and mustered a smile. 'Right now I have a play to rehearse.' He headed outside, and to avoid meeting Farr he went to check on the fire he'd put out. Then he walked around the back of the saloon.

Trinity and a few people from the mob had joined up with Jessica and Wallace beside the depot. He couldn't see Buck. Trinity and Wallace were talking as they walked along, while Jessica was lagging behind them and looking back towards the old part of town. When she saw Nimrod she put a hand to her heart to show she was relieved before she hurried on to walk with the others.

When Nimrod reached the depot Trinity's group had disappeared into town. Then, aside from several groups that had gathered in town and were engaged in intense conversation, he saw little sign that a major incident had just taken place. When he went into the theatre there was even less sign that anything was untoward, as Haywood was instructing his actors in the same way he always did.

Lawrence Saunders wasn't watching the rehearsal, so Nimrod clambered up on to the stage and moved to the position he'd adopted before. As he knelt down, Haywood looked at him with disdain.

'You're late,' he said.

'I'm sorry,' Nimrod said. 'I was unavoidably detained due to nearly being killed during the brawl that erupted in the old town when half the town joined forces to free Mayor Tucker.'

Nimrod's sarcasm only made Haywood shrug in a distracted way as if he hadn't been listening and was unaware of the events elsewhere in town. As the actors also showed no sign that they'd registered what he'd said, with a bemused smile Nimrod settled down on the stage and tried to relax after the recent chaos.

When the rehearsal started he listened to the play, but whereas during the previous rehearsal he'd enjoyed following it, this time it bored him. After getting a clue that Trinity might have killed Clayton, Haywood's version of the truth felt even more divorced from what had probably happened five years before.

By the end of the first act, Nimrod's boredom had grown into irritation. When he was allowed to stand up he strode back and forth across the stage as he loosened his cramped leg muscles.

'That was almost perfect,' Haywood proclaimed with a clap of his hands. 'With just one more rehearsal day before the grand opening, you're on course to captivate our audience.'

As Haywood had frequently interrupted the play with complaints and amendments, Nimrod presumed he was trying to bolster everyone's confidence, but the platitude still annoyed him.

'With lies,' he murmured to himself.

He must have spoken louder than he'd intended to, as Haywood turned to him.

'If you have a suggestion, we'd all welcome hearing it,' he said.

Nimrod knew he ought to keep his thoughts to himself, but he still found himself replying.

'This play is nonsense. You claim it gets to the truth, and yet it has nothing to do with what's really going on. Today there was a riot in the Hard Trails saloon brought about by some people reckoning they're missing out and by those who are prospering reckoning the others are no good. That's the truth of this town.'

Haywood shrugged. 'That is *a* truth, but it's not an interesting one. There are always squabbles.'

'I've only been here for a few days and four men have died, and that's more than squabbling, and more real than anything in your play.'

Haywood sighed and headed across the stage to stand in front of Nimrod, who set his hands on his hips.

'The main characters are content, and Lawrence is in Black Creek fetching Alexander Caldwell so he can see the play tomorrow. Yet you, a man who has only just arrived in town, want changes.'

'Maybe I'm not as qualified as others are, but I've understood more about Hopeman Town than you have.'

Haywood snorted a laugh. 'I guess that belief means you're becoming a proper actor. You're being temperamental and demanding rewrites.'

The actors laughed, but Nimrod only pointed at Haywood.

'Quit trying to make a joke out of this. If you wanted to, you could put some reality into this play.'

'Perhaps I could, but this is my play and my aims are different to whatever motivated the people to riot.'

Nimrod snorted an ironic laugh and stepped up closer to Haywood.

'You're wrong. Your aims are identical. You're ignoring the past to create a new future, and Trinity was destroying the last remnant of the old town for the same reason, except today he promised to let the old town survive. If he can compromise, perhaps you should, too.'

Haywood opened his mouth to refute Nimrod's statement, but then with a dismissive wave of the hand he turned away and gestured for the actors to get into their positions for the second act.

Nimrod glared at Haywood's back, but accepted that he'd wasted his breath and that he'd probably waste the rest of the afternoon if he continued to lie on the floor playing dead. He walked across the stage and jumped down, then without a backward glance, headed for the door.

Haywood uttered a comment about thin-skinned actors which raised another laugh, and before Nimrod had even reached the door an actor was delivering his next lines. Nimrod stormed on, but when he reached the outside door he recalled Haywood's comment that Lawrence was in Black Creek. He stopped, and then, as Haywood and his actors were probably the only other people in the theatre, he set about locating Lawrence's office.

So far he'd been cautious in investigating Lawrence's activities, but now he had an excellent opportunity to pry. He also reckoned that with his watcher being in the theatre earlier and with Buck's revelation that he was a detective, both his investigations were probably linked.

He headed down the corridor that ran beside the auditorium. Several rooms were at the end, one of which turned out to be an office. He stopped in the doorway and considered the room, while he turned his thoughts to how he could prove Trinity's belief that Lawrence was dishonest. Then he stepped inside.

Hearing movement behind him, he turned while ducking down, and so managed to avoid a wild blow from a man who had been standing behind the door. While his assailant was off balance, he grabbed the man's flailing arm at the elbow and twisted it behind his back. A moment later he'd mashed the man's face up against the wall and was holding him securely.

'I wasn't doing nothing,' the man said.

'Hubert Latham?' Nimrod said, now recognizing his opponent.

'Yeah.' Hubert relaxed his shoulders and glanced to the side. 'What are you doing here, Nimrod?'

'The same as you: not doing nothing.'

Hubert snorted a laugh, but he didn't reply until Nimrod had released his arm and stepped back.

'The man we talked about has been watching me, too, so I decided to take matters into my own hands while I still could. I've stayed in company so he can't catch me alone, but when I saw him leave the theatre earlier I figured this might be his base.'

'I'd reached the same conclusion, although I don't know why he came here.' Nimrod looked around the office. 'If we're lucky, we might find a clue.'

'Yeah, but we need to be quick. He went to watch that skirmish in the old town, so he could be back soon.'

Nimrod nodded and walked across the office to stand behind the desk.

'He did more than watch. He tried to burn down the Hard Trails saloon.'

Hubert sighed. 'The more I hear about him, the less I understand about what he wants.'

'What have you heard about him?'

Nimrod waited, but Hubert didn't reply, so he turned around to find that Hubert was facing the doorway. When Nimrod looked in that direction he couldn't help but wince.

The man they were discussing was standing in the doorway with a gun aimed at Hubert's chest.

CHAPTER 11

'So now we've established that the theatre is your base,' Nimrod said.

'I guess I told you to act like a detective,' the man said, his comment making Hubert glance at Nimrod, although he didn't look surprised.

'I am, and I'll figure out the rest before long.'

'You won't. The best you can do is to blunder your way in here while Lawrence is away. Detectives ought to be sneakier than that.' The man snorted. 'Even that Pinkerton knows that, even if he's being no more successful.'

'So you don't work with Buck?'

The man chuckled and with a steady step, walked into the office.

'We've met and exchanged threats, but that question shows you aren't very good at detecting. You should try something else, like acting, although you could do with more experience of death before you play a dead man again.'

The man winked. Then he fired, his shot slicing into Hubert's chest and making him stumble backwards for a pace. He blasted a second shot into his forehead, which downed him.

In response Nimrod jerked his hand towards his holster, but he had yet to touch leather when the man swung his gun to the side and aimed at him.

'What are you waiting for?' Nimrod asked when long seconds had passed without his opponent firing.

'I'm waiting for Haywood to tear himself away from his nonsense to do something about the gunfire in the theatre, and that'll be to fetch Marshal Farr.' The man took a step backwards towards the door. 'Then the marshal will find you standing beside a dead body and you'll face a problem.'

'He already knows someone killed people close to me, so I reckon I can answer his questions.'

The man laughed loudly. 'You've impressed me for the first time. You said that without laughing.'

Nimrod conceded the point with a shrug.

'Farr may not be a diligent lawman, but I had no reason to kill Hubert, and I guess you had plenty.'

The man raised a hand to his ear and cocked his head to one side. He nodded.

'People are coming. So it's time for me to go.' He

backed away into the doorway and glanced down the corridor before he faced Nimrod again. 'Be sure to tell Farr your story that someone else killed Hubert.'

The man stood poised ready to make good his escape, his smirk suggesting he wanted Nimrod to respond so he could goad him for one last time. Nimrod merely looked at him as he tried to work out why this man was so confident he would get away without recriminations.

An idea came to him. It was fantastical, but it fitted the facts and half-truths he'd learnt so far, and it was one that was so shocking he couldn't stop himself from wincing.

'I won't tell him *someone* killed Hubert. I'll tell him Ezra Howe did it.'

The man's right eye twitched, possibly confirming this assumption was correct, but he countered with the words: 'Ezra killed Leopold Hopeman, but everyone says he was shot in Black Creek. . . .'

The man Nimrod presumed was Ezra tailed off, letting Nimrod complete the thought:

'And everyone says Marshal Farr killed him, a lawman whom you reckon won't believe you killed Hubert. As everything that's happened recently has been designed to wipe the events of five years ago from history, that means you are Ezra, a man who—'

'That's a mighty big assumption,' Ezra snapped while gesturing at Nimrod angrily. 'And it just cost you your life.'

Ezra raised his gun to aim at Nimrod's head, while Nimrod ducked away in self-preservation. He couldn't hope to avoid a bullet, but when Ezra fired, the slug kicked his hat brim, his anger seemingly compromising his aim.

Nimrod dived to the floor behind the desk. Another shot kicked splinters from the wood, but by then Nimrod was behind the cover of the desk, where he drew his gun, slapping it on the top of the desk. He fired blind, but that didn't provoke any retaliatory gunfire, so he risked glancing up: Ezra was no longer in the doorway, so he jumped to his feet and sprinted across the office.

He stopped beside the door, and with his back to the wall, listened, hearing footfalls heading towards the back of the theatre. He dashed through the door and aimed his gun down the corridor.

Ezra was thirty feet away and fleeing. Nimrod aimed at his back, but Ezra must have heard him, as he turned and, while moving backwards, raised his gun, forcing Nimrod to step aside. Both men fired, their shots wild. Then Ezra reached the end of the corridor and moved round the corner.

Nimrod didn't know the layout at the back of the theatre, so he walked sideways with his back to the wall. When he could see down the next corridor he faced several doors, but only one was open, and shadows were moving beyond the doorway.

He aimed at the door, and a moment later a man stepped through, but with a groan of irritation Nimrod didn't fire as it was Haywood, who thrust his hands up high while taking a step backwards.

'Don't shoot,' he said.

'Someone was lurking in Lawrence's office and we exchanged gunfire before he fled,' Nimrod said. 'Did you see him?'

Haywood shook his head. Then he lowered his arms and glanced around before pointing at a door.

'Most of these rooms contain props and costumes. That's the only door that leads outside.'

This door was slightly ajar, but Nimrod didn't pursue Ezra as Ezra had a significant lead on him, and he had to deal with Hubert's body.

'He's probably long gone, but you still need to check out the other rooms.' Nimrod turned away. 'I'll make sure he didn't steal anything from Lawrence's office.'

Haywood gulped and made no immediate move to carry out Nimrod's order, but Nimrod still hurried back down the corridor to the office. Hubert had died from two messy wounds, but he'd collapsed on to a rug set before the desk, so Nimrod bundled him up in the rug.

He found a side room to the office that contained only stacked-up furniture, and which was dusty enough to suggest it wasn't often used. He gathered up the rug and the body in it, and deposited it behind a large chest so it was out of view from the door; then he went in search of Haywood.

When he found him, he and the actors were looking through the other rooms. Nimrod reported that nothing was amiss, and despite the incident Haywood wanted to resume the rehearsal as soon as possible. Nimrod encouraged him to remain calm, and left the theatre. He walked briskly through town while keeping an eye out for Ezra, but he didn't see him, and Marshal Farr wasn't in the law office either.

He headed to the Hard Trails saloon where Sydney was still exchanging opinions with the men who had been overwhelmed during the earlier incident. Sydney greeted him warmly before providing the unsurprising news that despite the deaths, Farr wouldn't take the matter further.

'It makes me wonder what sort of crime would concern him,' Sydney said, finishing off his story.

'I reckon I know,' Nimrod said. 'So I need your help.'

'If it helps to get Trinity, I'll do anything you ask.'

Nimrod nodded and urged Sydney to join him at the bar so they could talk privately.

'I reckon I can find out who killed Clayton, but the culprit could still be Trinity, Wallace, Jessica, Alexander or Lawrence Saunders, who was in town at the time. It could even be Ezra Howe.'

Sydney glanced aside and then shook his head.

'Trinity is the most likely killer, and Ezra died before my father did.'

'As we're learning, everything we've been told is wrong. Ezra is still alive. He's the one who shot Reed and Pablo, presumably because they'd joined you, and he's been watching me. He tried to burn down this saloon, and in the theatre just now he killed Hubert Latham.'

'Why?' Sydney gasped, his incredulous expression showing he was so surprised that he was struggling to speak.

'Hubert was the only other witness to his activities. Ezra wanted to blame the death on me and he sounded confident he'd succeed, which suggests he's in cahoots with Marshal Farr.'

'What do you want me to do?' Sydney asked as he regained his composure.

'I reckon Ezra will tell Farr that Hubert's dead, and he'll investigate, so we need to get rid of the body. I can distract everyone at the theatre. I hope you can do the rest.'

Sydney nodded. 'You can rely on me.'

Nimrod thanked him before explaining where he'd hidden the body. Then he left the saloon first and headed back to town.

When he entered the theatre, the rehearsal had

resumed. He slipped through the actors and lay down on stage, gathering no comment from Haywood despite the earlier incident. An hour passed quietly and the rehearsal was nearing the climax of the play when the actors tailed off. Nimrod glanced up to find that Marshal Farr had arrived.

'I've been dealing with the aftermath of the trouble in the old town,' Farr said. 'But I gather you had some trouble, too.'

'It wasn't anything we couldn't handle,' Haywood said, before gesturing at the actors to continue.

Farr stood with his hands on his hips showing his surprise at the reception he'd received, so Nimrod lowered his head. When he next glanced up, Farr had gone. He presumed that Farr then searched the theatre, as fifteen minutes later he returned and coughed to get Haywood's attention.

Only a few lines of the play had to be delivered, so Haywood silenced him with a raised hand and let the actors finish. Then he clapped his hands while offering congratulations and suggestions for improvements, his delay making Farr mutter to himself.

'I didn't find anything amiss,' Farr reported when Haywood at last turned to him.

'You sound disappointed,' Haywood said with a smile that only made Farr shake his head.

Farr turned away, but not before he glanced at

Nimrod, probably confirming he had followed Ezra's instructions to look for a body in the office. As he clearly hadn't found it, Nimrod allowed himself a contented smile before getting up.

Haywood then ordered a break before they rehearsed again. This would be the last chance they'd get before performing in front of Alexander tomorrow, and then before a paying audience the next day. Nobody complained, but Nimrod reckoned he'd spent enough time on matters that didn't help his investigations, so he made his excuses.

At the door he considered the merits of completing the task he'd started earlier versus the risk that Farr might return and find him, but he figured that time was running out for him to make headway. He headed to Lawrence's office, where he took a look to confirm that the body was no longer in the side room, then began rooting around.

Most of the cupboards and the desk drawers were unlocked, but he found a safe hidden in a cabinet that was large enough to contain something important. The safe resisted his inexpert attempts to open it, so he searched the rest of the office.

He found nothing of interest, so he tried to open the safe locks. They were secure, but later he found a key that opened a drawer, and tucked under a pile of innocuous documents was a ledger. This contained details of income and expenditure since the theatre had opened three years before – and unless the records were false they painted a picture of an establishment that was in trouble.

Costs were high, with one large regular payment that wasn't described, while income was low and sporadic, depending on what the theatre was showing. The only reliable source of income were donations from the Legacy Fund, which appeared to be keeping the business going.

Feeling that he'd learnt everything he could in the office, he tidied up and then left the theatre using the route Ezra had taken. It was now early evening, so figuring that only one person would be prepared to answer the questions that the events of that day had raised, he headed to his hotel.

He went up to Jessica's room and knocked, receiving a terse demand that he wait, although when she opened the door and saw who was there she softened her tone and invited him in.

'I'd hoped you'd seek me out,' she said, while fluffing her hair. 'I want you to know I'm relieved you weren't harmed today.'

'I'm pleased you care,' Nimrod said. 'Now show it by telling me why Trinity really hired me.'

CHAPTER 12

'Trinity wants you to find out if Lawrence Saunders is cheating us,' Jessica said, while not meeting Nimrod's eye.

She headed to a chair by the window and sat down. Then she invited Nimrod to sit opposite her.

'That's what Trinity would want you to say, but we've been close,' Nimrod said. He sat down and leaned forward to take her hand. 'So tell me why he needed me. He was calm today when his life was in danger, so I reckon he could sort out any problems by himself, even without Buck's help.'

'There are some tasks a mayor can't be seen to do, and despite my concerns about Buck's behaviour I'll admit he has his uses, but uncovering the truth about Lawrence isn't one of them.'

Her tone had sounded honest, so he gave a reassuring smile.

'I welcome your confidence in me, but you're keeping something from me. I will find out what that is, and if we're to continue to see each other, it'd be better if you told me.'

'Not all secrets are kept to deceive.' She gripped his hand tightly. 'Don't make me give you an answer.'

'Now that I know there's a secret, I can't let this matter go.'

She loosened her grip and looked out of the window. She sighed, and when she spoke again her voice was low and sad.

'My husband didn't collapse in a fit of rage. He was strangled, and we suspect Lawrence did it, but after all these years it can never be proved, so Trinity is doing the next best thing by proving he's cheating the town fund.'

'Why are you sure it was Lawrence and not Trinity, or even Wallace?'

She turned back to him and looked him in the eye.

'When Clayton's body was found I was in a bedroom with Wallace.' She waited until he raised an eyebrow and then softened her declaration with a smile. 'Nothing untoward had taken place, but we'll never know if something could have happened, as Trinity found us. I pleaded with him not to tell my husband. As they were friends he refused, but when he went to Clayton he was dead.'

117

'Why did he suspect Lawrence?'

She shrugged. 'Clayton had been dead for a while, so it could have been anyone, but Lawrence was just about the only other person in town aside from Marshal Farr.'

'I didn't know the marshal was here back then.'

'After his success in finding Ezra Howe, Farr wanted to be a lawman in a boom town. He had found Trinity standing over Clayton's body, so the situation looked bad for Trinity, but Trinity talked him round by offering him the position of marshal.'

Jessica gnawed at her bottom lip, so Nimrod gave her hand a comforting pat.

'I'd guess Trinity now regrets that.'

She nodded. 'Despite Trinity's suspicions, Farr didn't reckon Lawrence did it.'

'Which might suggest Farr killed Clayton.'

'We don't think so. Farr turns a blind eye to trouble when it suits him, so we suspect Lawrence bought his freedom with the promise of a cut of the money he wanted to build his theatre, but we couldn't do anything about it as we were trapped in a circle of deceit.'

Nimrod thought this through, and then smiled.

'If you didn't give Lawrence money, he couldn't pay Farr, and Farr would get annoyed and accuse Trinity?'

'That was our dilemma, so we put aside the issue and made this town prosper – but now the time has come to put things right. If Farr were to claim now that Trinity killed Clayton, we reckon nobody would believe him.'

Nimrod nodded. 'Enough time should have passed, and Trinity's behaviour today showed the townsfolk he's a decent man.'

Jessica nodded. 'And Haywood's play reinforces our version of events, an irony I hope Lawrence appreciates when we defeat him.'

'Thank you for that,' he said.

He squeezed her hand, but she didn't repay him in kind.

'I told you because you said only the truth could keep us together.' She hardened her expression and slipped her hand away. 'So now it's your turn. Tell me what you're not telling me.'

For long moments Nimrod looked at her, and when she met his gaze he spoke up while studying her expression.

'Clayton's son Sydney also reckons his father was murdered, and he asked me to find the killer. When I read your husband's journal I thought it was Lawrence. Then I thought it was Trinity. Now I reckon Lawrence got the watcher your husband wrote about to do it.'

'Who is he?' she snapped, her voice breaking.

Nimrod narrowed his eyes. 'I reckon you already know. You've revealed plenty of information, but the

119

fact that Lawrence has a hired gun is the secret you didn't want to tell me.'

She closed her eyes and when she opened them they were watering.

'If you act on that knowledge you'll be killed, and I don't want that to happen. Leave it to Buck to deal with him in his own way.'

'So that's why Trinity hired Buck: to get this other man.'

'Wallace hired him. It's just about the only useful thing he's done since we inherited Hopeman's legacy.'

Nimrod glanced aside as the last piece of the puzzle fitted into place.

'In that case, I'll let Buck complete his mission.'

She breathed a sigh of relief. Then, as if that show of emotion wasn't enough, she laughed and spread her hands.

'And that's all of it. Now there are no more secrets between us.'

He shook his head. 'There's one final matter. Lawrence's hired gun is Ezra Howe.'

She put a hand to her mouth and looked at him until he nodded.

'We never suspected that Marshal Farr lied about killing Ezra.'

'Lawrence must have known Leopold was wealthy and got Ezra to kill him. When he didn't get his hands on his money, he came here to try again.'

'I agree, and I'll have to tell Wallace and Trinity.' She gulped. 'And if Sydney is in town I'll have to speak with him, too.'

Nimrod frowned. 'You should delay seeing him until after Ezra has been defeated. Even then it'll be an uncomfortable meeting, but it won't be as tricky as when I tell him I'm involved with you.'

'That will be awkward.' She put a hand on his knee. 'But being involved with me does have its benefits.'

'It does,' he said with a smile.

Nimrod stayed in the hotel until a few minutes to noon the next day, the time Haywood had told him to report for the performance in front of Alexander Caldwell. Since hearing Jessica's revelations the previous day, and sharing his information, he had decided to stay out of the way while she talked with Wallace and Trinity, although he felt guilty about not seeing Sydney and telling him about the recent information he'd learnt.

When he went to the dressing room he was given a new jacket and a large hat for him to place in front of his face to help mask any movements he might make.

Haywood was giving his actors last minute instructions, so Nimrod headed on to the stage, but he couldn't see if Lawrence was with Alexander as the curtains were closed. The stage had also been dressed with a depiction of a saloon rather than the usual minimal props.

Nimrod sat down in his usual position. For the first time the prospect of spending the next two hours lying immobile made him feel weary, but he consoled himself with the thought that Jessica reckoned Trinity would soon confront Lawrence, and after that he could stop pretending to be an actor.

Presently Haywood arrived and peered out between the curtains. He nodded to someone and then gestured for Nimrod to lie down.

Then, with a swish of the curtains, the play got underway. For a while Nimrod stayed still, but when his arms and legs complained, he shifted position while using the movement to glance up and see who was in the audience. His hat blocked his view of most of the auditorium, but as promised, Alexander was in the front row with Lawrence and Marshal Farr sitting on one side of him, and Haywood on the other. These men appeared to be the only members of the audience, other than a solitary man sitting near the back.

Nimrod watched this man, fearing he might be Ezra, but when the man shuffled in his seat he realized with concern that it was Sydney. Worse, he reckoned Sydney wasn't moving around because he was uncomfortable, but because of the content of the play, which he hadn't been warned about.

The current scene involved an argument between Alexander and Clayton, with Alexander being reasonable and Clayton raging.

Worse would come during the second act when Clayton would become so angry he would keel over and die, but Nimrod wasn't surprised when Sydney jumped to his feet and gestured angrily at the stage. Then he headed along between the seats.

Nimrod hoped he would leave the theatre, but instead he made his way towards the stage.

'This play is all lies,' he shouted, although not loudly enough to interrupt the play, so he drew his gun and fired into the high ceiling. 'It's making out Clayton was a troublemaker.'

As the actors broke off from enacting their argument and turned to Sydney, Haywood jumped to his feet and moved to intercept him.

'This is a private showing,' he said. 'Come along tomorrow when as a paying member of the audience you'll have the right to complain. Either way, you'll do that complaining without your gun.'

'I have more right to complain than anyone else here does.'

Haywood shook his head, but Alexander stood up and patted his shoulder.

'This man is no friend of mine, but he has a point,'

he said. 'Even if he's not prepared to disclose his reasoning, you should listen to him.'

'It's too late to listen to critics. This play will be performed tomorrow in front of—'

'It won't unless I give my approval,' Alexander snapped. 'That was what we agreed, and on reflection, having seen how you've portrayed the incidents I was involved in, I won't.'

As Sydney murmured his thanks and moved to holster his gun, Haywood waved his arms in agitation, which encouraged Marshal Farr to stand up and join in the argument.

'This man was holding the mayor hostage yesterday,' he declared. 'Nobody should side with him.'

'Stay out of this,' Sydney said.

Sydney kept his gun drawn and with it thrust out before him he advanced on the marshal, making Farr twitch his hand towards his gun while Alexander moved to intercept Sydney.

A gunshot blasted, the sound echoing in the auditorium. Then Alexander stumbled a pace before keeling over with a hand rising to clutch his bloodied chest.

'You shot him!' Farr declared. 'Drop that gun or I'll—'

'I never fired,' Sydney said.

He looked with incredulity at Alexander, who rolled over to lie on his back and then became still.

Haywood stared at Sydney with horror, while Lawrence stood up and edged his hand towards his gun.

As it was clear that these people either believed or would support Farr's declaration, Nimrod looked at the actors – but they were backing away, suggesting they thought Sydney had killed Alexander.

Thankfully Nimrod had seen that Sydney hadn't fired his gun. Then again, nobody else he was aware of could have shot Alexander either. He looked into all corners of the auditorium and as he saw nobody, he finished his consideration of the scene facing Sydney and the dead Alexander. He recalled how Alexander had been standing when he'd been shot, and as Sydney was in the right position to have been the shooter, the killer must have been behind Sydney.

Nimrod got up and hurried to the front of the stage, making Sydney and the others watch him. Then he looked at the area where the shooter must have been standing.

Two sets of box seats were above the side of the stage, but the actors would have seen anyone who had used them. The floor between the stage and the seats was open, with no cover for someone to hide behind, and the nearest door was close enough that they would have heard anyone using it to escape.

He jumped down from the stage and stood behind

Sydney with his back to him. He faced a decorated length of wall, and the corridor along which he had chased Ezra would be on the other side of the wall.

With a determined tread he set off, making Haywood speak up.

'What's wrong?' he called after him.

Nimrod figured that if he explained, Lawrence and Farr would stop him before he uncovered the truth, so he kept walking until he reached the wall. Then he fingered the decorations until he found a depiction of a face in which one eye was a hole he could see through to, presumably, the corridor.

The hole was large enough for someone on the other side to see the audience, so it was also large enough to accommodate a gun barrel.

Nimrod headed towards the door that stood beside the stage. Lawrence and Farr were looking at him with open-mouthed alarm, which suggested they kncw the significance of his discovery.

Then the two men looked at each other and nodded, the result of their silent exchange of views becoming apparent when Lawrence chased after Nimrod and Farr gestured for Sydney to drop his gun. Nimrod didn't see the result of this confrontation as by then he had reached the door.

He pushed through it, and as he'd expected, emerged into the corridor near to Lawrence's office. The doorway that led outside was to his right, but as it was closed he headed to the left to confirm his theory that the shooter had been outside the auditorium.

He hurried past the corner of the corridor only to skid to a halt when he proved his theory in the most irrefutable manner possible: Ezra Howe was in front of him, and was already aiming a gun at him.

CHAPTER 13

'That was some mighty fine reasoning,' Ezra said.

'It was easy to work out how you did it, but not why,' Nimrod said.

'A decent detective should be able to figure it out.'

Nimrod looked at the corner of the corridor to work out how he could dive for cover quickly, but that option was removed when Lawrence came through the door. Lawrence smirked as he appraised Nimrod and then drew his gun.

'We know that Trinity plans to move against us,' Lawrence said. 'So we're moving against him first. Alexander's dead, Clayton's son has been dealt with, and the rest will soon follow.'

'How do you know about Clayton's son?'

'We know everything that goes on, despite none of us being detectives. Now the only question is whether you're of any further use to us.'

As Lawrence aimed his gun at Nimrod's chest, behind him the outside door swung open and Buck slipped through. Buck wouldn't be able to see Ezra, but he noted the scene without any apparent surprise.

'Ezra's holding a gun on me from one side and you're on the other side,' Nimrod said. 'So I guess I've got no choice but to cooperate.'

Lawrence sighed, suggesting he thought Nimrod's statement had been designed to buy time, but it had the desired effect when Buck backed away through the door.

It would take Buck about two minutes to run around the outside of the theatre and sneak up on Ezra, the most dangerous of Nimrod's two opponents, from behind, and thankfully Lawrence started using up that time when he replied.

'I know you won't cooperate, but we could use you in the same way that Farr is using Sydney.' Lawrence took a step forwards. 'What did you do with Hubert's body?'

'I'll tell you, but we need to talk about other matters first.'

Lawrence chuckled. 'You're playing for time because you heard a noise behind me and you reckon someone is coming to help you – but you're wrong.'

Lawrence glanced back down the corridor, and

with impeccable timing Sydney came through the door to the auditorium with his hands raised and with Marshal Farr a step behind him. Sydney was scowling, and that scowl deepened when he saw Nimrod.

'You got me into this mess,' he said, pointing at Nimrod. 'You let Haywood write lies about Clayton.'

'I kept some of what I learnt in my investigation a secret, but for good reason,' Nimrod said.

'Nothing excuses you. . . .' Sydney's retort tailed off as he appeared to notice for the first time that Lawrence was holding Nimrod at gunpoint. 'What's going on here?'

Farr snarled a warning to be quiet, and pushed Sydney on towards Lawrence.

'It seems we've lost,' Nimrod said. 'So the truth about who killed Clayton will never come out, but at least we'll have the satisfaction of knowing that—'

'No more talk,' Lawrence muttered. 'This ends here.'

Lawrence aimed his gun at Sydney, clearly expecting that Ezra would deal with Nimrod. So Nimrod set off towards the corner of the corridor, but he had moved for only a pace when a gunshot blasted.

Nimrod winced, but then found to his relief that he was unharmed, so while drawing his gun he glanced over his shoulder. Buck was standing at the far end of the corridor while Ezra was arching his back, suggesting that he hadn't fired and that Buck had shot him.

Nimrod stopped and snapped his gun round to aim at Ezra. His opponent righted himself and with a pained expression he fired at Nimrod, but in his weakened state his shot winged past Nimrod's left arm. Then Nimrod hammered lead low into Ezra's stomach, making him double over.

Ezra still teetered round on the spot and moved to shoot at Buck, but Buck and Nimrod fired simultaneous shots that downed him. As Buck broke into a run down the corridor, Nimrod turned to find that Sydney had accosted Farr and now the two men were struggling.

Lawrence must have kept half an eye on Nimrod as he swung his gun away from Sydney to aim at him.

'This does end here,' Nimrod said. 'Ezra is dead and that removes all your firepower.'

'You're wrong,' Lawrence said. 'And you've got so much else wrong already.'

Lawrence smirked, enjoying gloating on the situation, but Nimrod made him pay for his over-confidence: with a quick snap of the hand he raised his gun and blasted a slug into Lawrence's chest.

Lawrence wasted a shot into the wall to Nimrod's side while he stumbled backwards for a pace. A second shot to the chest downed him.

While reloading Nimrod ran towards Sydney and Farr. He reached them as Farr dragged himself away from his opponent, but an alarmed expression overcame the marshal's face. A moment later Nimrod saw the reason for his shock: Sydney had wrested the marshal's gun off him. A moment later he sliced lead into Farr's side.

Farr dropped to his knees before he keeled over to the side. Through pained eyes he looked at Sydney.

'Lawrence can't answer, but you can,' Sydney said, looming up over the shot man. 'Who killed Clayton Jones?'

Farr sneered. Then his expression changed to a grimace of pain. He rolled over on to his back and wheezed a shallow breath through gritted teeth.

'You're not getting any answers out of me,' Farr murmured as he cast a defiant glare at Sydney. Buck then ran around the corner where he took in the scene with a raised eyebrow.

'Three months of investigating and it's all over in three minutes,' he said with a light tone.

'It's not over yet,' Nimrod said. 'We still don't know which one of these varmints killed Clayton.'

Buck shrugged. 'I was only hired to bring down Lawrence's hired gun. With your help, I've done that.'

'It's never as simple as that. Three men are dead, and we need an explanation for what's just happened.'

Buck shook his head and he continued shaking it even when Sydney spoke up.

'That's four dead men,' he said. 'Marshal Farr isn't breathing no more.'

'Don't worry,' Nimrod said. 'You killed a lawman, but he was corrupt.'

'Are you saying he covered up the truth about Clayton's death?'

'I'm saying that could be the least of it. Lawrence might have killed Clayton, or he could have got Ezra to do it.' Nimrod sighed. 'Farr could even have done it himself, but whatever the answer, these three conspired to hide the truth and to profit from it.'

Sydney lowered his head, and when it didn't look as if he'd reply, Buck joined Nimrod.

'You two stay here until I've rounded up Trinity and the others. They'll decide how we'll deal with this, and rest assured they'll find a way.'

He gave a brief smile, and when Nimrod nodded he headed back down the corridor.

'So Buck reckons this is over now,' Sydney said after a while, his voice flat. He looked up at Nimrod. 'Do you?'

'You hired me to get answers and I've narrowed it down to three possibilities. That might be the best I can do, but I haven't given up hope that one day I'll get a definitive answer.'

Sydney looked at the bodies while shaking his head.

'And I suppose you reckon I should be grateful you've told me that much?'

Nimrod sighed. 'I did keep information from you. Then again I told Trinity very little about my activities because that's how I usually—'

'Quit with the excuses!' Sydney snapped.

Nimrod spread his hands, conceding Sydney's point.

'You're right. I'm making excuses. I didn't tell you about Haywood's play or about what I'd worked out because I was worried you'd react badly – but perhaps that was a mistake.'

'You're sure right it was a mistake.' Sydney walked around Farr's body and moved on to stand over Lawrence. 'What made you suspect them?'

Nimrod gnawed his bottom lip, finding he couldn't tell him that Jessica had provided most of his vital information.

'I've been trying to keep an open mind, but we should wait until Trinity returns and fills in the gaps.'

Sydney nodded and faced Nimrod.

'We should, but I need to do something first.'

Nimrod waited for an explanation, but Sydney merely glared at him. Then, a moment before Sydney acted, he saw the anger in his eyes and knew what he was about to do, but he didn't defend himself and so a swinging punch to the jaw sent him reeling into the wall.

Nimrod groaned as he dropped down into a sitting position. Then he looked up at Sydney, who spat on the floor before walking away.

Trinity looked triumphant as Buck talked him through the incident in the corridor. They had gathered in the auditorium. The actors had gone backstage while Trinity, Jessica and Wallace decided upon their next actions.

Trinity was standing in front of the stage. The bodies, with their jackets over their faces, were lined up before him. Jessica and Wallace sat together on the front row with Haywood, Nimrod and Buck a few seats away. Sydney had slumped down in a chair ten rows back from the stage where he eyed everyone with undisguised irritation.

'Everybody knows Farr was ineffective, and many know about a mystery gunman,' Trinity said when Buck had finished. 'The fact that he was Ezra Howe proves Farr's dishonesty, but nobody has ever spoken ill of Lawrence, so this needs careful thought.'

Trinity looked at Wallace and Jessica for a response. Wallace didn't meet his eye, leaving Jessica to lean forwards.

'We've had five years of trouble because the truth was covered up,' she said. 'If that happens again, it could cause us just as much trouble.'

'Are you saying we tell everyone what happened?'

'We don't need to tell the townsfolk anything, but neither should we deny the truth. We should just report there's been a shooting. Then we recruit a new marshal. We'll tell him Ezra worked for Lawrence, and let him reach his own conclusion, that Nimrod and Buck were justified in killing them.'

Trinity looked at Nimrod and Buck. When they both uttered affirmative grunts, he rubbed his hands while nodding, but Sydney snorted and got to his feet.

'What about me?' he said. 'Will I be left to take the blame just like Clayton was made out to be in the wrong in the play?'

'No,' Trinity said. 'Everyone will support you in confirming that Ezra tried to make it look as if you shot Alexander.'

'Except I killed Marshal Farr. As you're all as bad as each other with your twisted versions of the truth, that's sure to have repercussions.'

Sydney glared at each person in turn, saving an especially long look for Jessica before he made his way along the seats and then walked to the door.

'He has a right to be angry,' Trinity said. 'I'll go after him and persuade him not to do anything foolish. Then I'll get the word out that there's been a shooting.'

With that, Trinity gestured for Buck to join him. When the two men headed to the door, Nimrod sat beside Jessica, making Wallace sneer at him for no reason he could see.

Haywood came over and stood before them. He rocked from foot to foot before he voiced his concern.

'Can my play still be performed tomorrow?' he asked with a small voice.

'I wish I could say otherwise, but it can,' Wallace said. 'The gunfight will be good for publicity.' He sighed, and with a slow shake of the head, sloped away to follow Trinity and Buck out of the door.

'But not so good for Sydney, or for those who like the truth,' Nimrod said.

'Sydney will just have to accept my version of events,' Haywood said.

'Except in your play Clayton keels over and dies, so nobody else will believe your version of events either, if and when the truth comes out that he was murdered.'

Haywood frowned. 'I guess I ought to make some last minute changes to the play.'

Nimrod stood up and slapped Haywood on the back.

'If you're prepared to do that, now that nobody needs to be defensive, perhaps you can introduce even more truth.'

Haywood shook his head, but to Nimrod's surprise Jessica spoke up.

'I'd welcome that,' she said. 'I'm sure Wallace and Trinity would, too.'

Haywood lowered his head. Then with a resigned sigh he looked up and faced her.

'What do you have in mind?' he asked.

CHAPTER 14

An hour before the first performance of *Hopeman's Legacy* was due to begin, Nimrod went to Jessica's room and passed on the good news.

'So that means you can accompany me,' Jessica said.

'I can,' Nimrod said. 'Haywood's changes mean I don't have to act no more.'

'Have you seen those changes?'

'No, but I don't reckon there's anything for you to worry about. He's taken your suggestion to include you and Wallace being friendly, he's taken out Clayton causing trouble, and he's ending the play with an agreement rather than Clayton's death.'

'I hope that's enough to placate Sydney.'

Nimrod smiled. 'I'm pleased you care about him, even if he doesn't want anything to do with you.'

'I'm doing what Clayton would have wanted me to

do. I don't want any more repercussions from the events of five years ago.' She sighed. 'To that end this morning Trinity spoke to Sydney. Oliver Peak rented the Hard Trails saloon from me, and Trinity offered to give Sydney the place. He accepted.'

'That was generous, but I'm surprised he agreed.'

'Trinity told him it was a gift from the fund rather than from me, but no matter. I hope that might build him a fresh start.'

'I hope so too, but the problem that might never go away is that even though we know Clayton's killer was one of three men, the truth was probably buried yesterday.'

Jessica nodded. Then she set about getting ready to leave, so Nimrod settled down to wait for her. Thirty minutes later they left the room and joined Trinity, Wallace and Buck downstairs. As always Wallace looked disinterested in proceedings, while Trinity smiled as he detailed his recent successes.

He had found a suitable town marshal, and while chatting with the townsfolk he had detected only contempt for Marshal Farr and indifference about Lawrence Saunders's demise. He didn't anticipate any problems, although the sombre expression on Buck's face suggested he didn't share Trinity's optimism.

Together they moved on to the theatre. In keeping with premières in Hopeman Town no great fuss was being made, although Trinity had decided that would change now that the fund would be running the business. So the group milled in with the people queuing to get in, which meant that for the next fifteen minutes Trinity shook numerous hands. He even exchanged pleasantries with people who had helped Oliver defend his saloon, as he made good his promise to seek reconciliation.

When they were inside they were directed to one of the four sets of box seats that were to the sides of the auditorium and looking down on the stage.

Nimrod sat on the end of the row of chairs beside Jessica and Wallace. Trinity stayed standing to wave to well-wishers, while Buck stood beside him and glared with suspicion at the audience.

'Trinity's been under strain for years,' Jessica said to Nimrod when she noted his expression was almost as irritated as Buck's was. 'Let him enjoy the moment now we're assured of a brighter future.'

'You and Wallace have been under the same strain,' Nimrod said. 'You're not behaving like that.'

'Maybe so, but we're not politicians.'

'You're not, which is probably why Buck's behaving as if he reckons theatres will never be a safe place for a politician.'

Jessica frowned. 'Buck's worried that Lawrence had another accomplice he hasn't uncovered yet.'

Nimrod gulped, as he hadn't been aware of this

possibility. Guns weren't allowed in the theatre, so Buck was at a disadvantage if someone had ignored the order.

'He's wise to be cautious, but I've seen nothing to suggest his concerns are warranted.'

Jessica smiled and settled back in her chair, but their conversation had caught Buck's attention and he came over to stand in front of them.

'That's the opinion of an ex-Pinkerton detective, is it?' he said with a surprising level of contempt.

'Ezra lurked in the shadows and he was formidable enough for Lawrence not to need anyone else.'

'Maybe he didn't, but after we defeated Lawrence I've heard accounts of Ezra's activities from people who were in Black Creek when Farr claimed he'd killed him. They confirmed they'd only heard the story he'd been killed, and they never saw a body.'

'That's reassuring.'

'It's not. I've also heard several different descriptions of Ezra.' Buck leaned forward and lowered his voice for emphasis. 'None of them describe the man we shot.'

Nimrod winced and then closed his eyes as he thought back to the time when he'd deduced the mystery gunslinger's identity. The man's aggressive reaction suggested he had made a correct identification, but he hadn't confirmed he was Ezra.

'So we might have killed another hired gun and

Ezra could still be alive?'

'Exactly, and until I know the full story, my mission isn't over.'

'If you're right, neither is mine.'

Buck nodded and when he rejoined Trinity to watch for trouble, Jessica looked at Nimrod with a worried expression. Nimrod gave her a reassuring smile, while Wallace slumped down in his chair with a weary sigh, although that could have been because the stage curtain was fluttering, hinting the play was about to start.

This development encouraged Trinity to sit down, but Buck stayed standing until Trinity told him to join him to avoid disconcerting anyone. Buck did as he'd been ordered, but he still sat forward in his chair, so Nimrod edged forwards to adopt the same posture.

Presently Haywood stood up from his seat in the front row, and with his arms raised, beckoned for quiet.

'*Hopeman's Legacy*, a play in two acts,' he announced simply.

He sat down. Then the curtains opened to reveal the saloon set. To Nimrod's surprise he felt a twinge of regret that he wasn't lying face down on the stage providing a dramatic focus to the story. He had heard the play several times, so while he watched for trouble, he listened only for Haywood's changes.

143

As it turned out, aside from the replacement of comments about the body lying in the saloon with a discussion about Leopold's recent death, the play started as it had done before.

With the audience watching the stage, Nimrod reckoned anyone behaving oddly would be easy to notice, so as the play progressed he found himself becoming swept along by the story. Later, Haywood's changes became obvious, with Clayton's role being less confrontational, while Alexander spoke many of the lines that had originally been written for Clayton.

When the curtains closed at the end of the first act, Jessica nodded with approval and Trinity also looked pleased, although Wallace had closed his eyes and was trying to doze. Buck insisted that everyone stay in the box during the intermission, and Trinity didn't object.

Everyone sat quietly for thirty minutes, the break making Jessica and Trinity join Wallace in becoming bored with proceedings. So when the play restarted Jessica was resting her head on Nimrod's shoulder and Trinity's eyes were glazed as he appeared to have his mind on other matters.

But their lack of interest didn't last for long, although strangely it was Wallace who first sat up straight and peered at the stage. Nimrod couldn't work out what had interested him, until he noted that the actors playing Jessica and Wallace were enacting a scene that had changed substantially from the one with which he was familiar.

The actors were debating the merits of Trinity's and Alexander's differing views on what they should do with the money, but Haywood had enlivened the scene with flirtatious comments. Their behaviour was in keeping with Jessica's suggestion, but it made Wallace rub his chin in an animated manner, while Trinity scowled.

Trinity's disapproval grew when the actor playing him interrupted Jessica and Wallace's cosy meeting, and took so much exception to what he'd overheard that he drew a gun. Then he held it on the other two while demanding to know what they were doing.

'Aside from the gun, this is too close to the truth,' Trinity said while standing up.

As the actor playing Trinity gestured extravagantly with his gun, Trinity glared down at Haywood. He failed to attract his attention, as Haywood was shaking his head, suggesting the actor was improvising and he didn't approve.

The other actors seemed to confirm this when they stumbled over their next lines.

'The main problem is that it's too melodramatic,' Jessica said.

'And it's not close to the truth,' Wallace said. 'Nothing like this ever happened.'

'It didn't, but it might have.'

Wallace swirled round to face Jessica, but Jessica ignored him as she continued to watch the actors. Trinity still glared at Haywood, but surprisingly Buck started watching the play for the first time.

'It's him,' he said.

Nimrod didn't know what he meant, but then the actor playing Trinity stopped gesturing with his gun and it just happened to be aimed up at their box. Buck jerked forward to stand in front of Trinity, making Nimrod work out what was happening.

The actor playing Trinity was Ezra Howe.

CHAPTER 15

Nimrod leapt to his feet, making Jessica rock to the side over his vacated seat. Then he clambered up on to the front of the box and stood with his arms spread wide for balance.

A ripple of consternation passed through the audience as everyone turned to look up at him. It also made the actor playing Trinity, whom he now knew to be Ezra Howe, stop the pretence and set his feet wide apart as he steadied his aim.

Nimrod leapt down. The box was around fifteen feet above the stage, and he fell for long enough to start worrying about whether he'd injure himself before he slammed down and then pitched forwards.

He went sprawling on to his front, coincidentally adopting the position he had taken during rehearsals, before he rolled and came up on one knee. He was facing Ezra, who was ignoring him as he took aim and then fired.

People in the audience cried out in panic, but Nimrod put them from his mind as he rose up and ran towards his opponent. Ezra fired a second time, again making people shout. Then Nimrod dived and slammed into him.

He hit Ezra in the side and knocked him down to the stage where they both skidded along for several feet before coming to a halt. Ezra squirmed, and because Nimrod had winded himself when he'd fallen, with a flailing of his arms and legs he freed himself.

Then Ezra ran across the stage towards the box, seemingly planning to clamber up the wall and gain access to it. Nobody was visible in the box, so Nimrod couldn't tell whether Ezra had harmed anyone.

He set off after his opponent. Nobody else tried to stop Ezra, who put a foot on to a ledge and raised a hand to pull himself up. He would need to use at least four more ledges before he reached the box, and it took him two attempts to rest a foot on the next foothold, giving Nimrod enough time to pound towards him and grab his leg. Nimrod tugged, but Ezra held on and kicked out.

Ezra's heel caught Nimrod's chin, making him tumble backwards to land on his back. He shook himself and looked up at Ezra, who smirked when he saw he'd knocked him away before he resumed climbing.

Nimrod got up; his repeated falls had jarred his limbs so he was slow to move, and by the time he reached the wall Ezra was out of his reach. He set off up the wall after him, taking the same route.

Each time he drew himself higher he looked up hoping he could grab a trailing foot, but Ezra was out of his reach. Then to his horror, his quarry rolled over into the box to disappear from sight.

Jessica shouted a warning and a moment later a gunshot blasted. With a heavy heart Nimrod continued clambering.

He gritted his teeth in anticipation of more gunshots, but he heard only scuffling noises. Three more frantic movements brought him up to the box.

He slapped a hand on the rim and dragged himself over it to come to rest in the box, standing crouched over. To his surprise Wallace was grappling with Ezra.

Jessica was kneeling beside Trinity, who was clutching a bloodied upper arm. Lying sprawled across his legs was Buck, his form still and the dark stain spreading across his chest showing he'd taken the lead that had been meant for Trinity.

Wallace had grabbed Ezra's gun arm and was holding it high to keep the gun aimed at the ceiling, but Ezra was getting the upper hand as he dragged the gun down towards Wallace's head.

Nimrod stood up straight and with long strides he

stepped up to Ezra, who saw him coming and redoubled his efforts to seize control of his gun. The weapon jerked down towards Wallace making him flinch away, but then Nimrod reached them and with a backhanded swipe he knocked Ezra aside.

Ezra stumbled into a chair and toppled over it to go clattering down on the other side, while Wallace stumbled a pace in the other direction. Wallace righted himself against the front of the box and grinned when he discovered he'd got hold of the gun.

With a confident movement he turned round and aimed the gun at the chair before walking forward to peer over it.

'Don't shoot him,' Nimrod said. He looked around the chair at the supine and defenceless Ezra. 'We need him alive to find out . . .'

He didn't need to end the sentence as Wallace planted two bullets in Ezra's chest, making him arch his back before he flopped back down.

'He came up here to kill us all,' Wallace reported as Ezra became still.

'We had to defend ourselves, but he was the last person who might have known something about Clayton's death and the events of five years ago.'

'I'm sure Jessica is pleased you'd have risked her life to get an answer.' Wallace pointed at his own chest. 'I did what was necessary.'

Wallace turned and held out a hand to help Jessica to her feet, but Jessica shook her head.

'The two of us getting close didn't happen five years ago, and it won't happen now,' she said.

With a glance at Trinity to confirm he didn't need any further assistance, she got up and walked around Wallace to join Nimrod, who patted her shoulder, an action that made Wallace firm his jaw.

'We need to get help for Trinity,' Nimrod said, and when she nodded he looked down into the auditorium where the audience was peering up at the box with concern.

Nimrod directed a placating gesture at them. Then he made to escort Jessica out of the box, but Wallace was standing in his path.

Previously Wallace hadn't got involved in anything, so Nimrod wondered why he had killed Ezra. He recalled that his change of attitude had occurred during a scene in the play where he and Jessica had flirted.

This thought made him stop.

'Come on,' Jessica said. 'You're right that Trinity needs help.'

Nimrod didn't reply immediately as he was still piecing together a theory about Wallace's recent behaviour, and when it reached a logical conclusion he looked at Wallace. His expression must have been more accusatory than he'd intended, as Wallace stepped backwards.

'Why are you looking at me like that?' he said.

'I'm wondering why you acted decisively for the first time I've seen,' Nimrod said calmly.

'Jessica was in danger.'

'That's what I thought.'

For long moments the two men faced each other. Then Jessica twitched, suggesting she'd had the same thought that had occurred to Nimrod.

'Are you saying it was him?' she murmured, turning to Nimrod.

Nimrod didn't need to answer when Wallace raised his gun and aimed it at him.

'Step away from her,' Wallace said levelly.

Nimrod raised his hands. 'So you're going to kill me like you killed Clayton, are you?'

'He didn't care for her as much as I do, and neither do you, so you're not leaving this theatre alive.'

'So Lawrence was paying Farr to keep silent about Leopold's death, not Clayton's?'

'Sure, but either way they all profited from the arrangement.'

'They were only able to profit because you had something to hide.'

Wallace snarled, but when he didn't reply Jessica spoke up.

'But no longer,' she said, her voice regaining its

usual assurance.

'Don't be so sure of that,' Wallace said. 'We can move on from this together and there's no need for—'

'You're deluded!'

Wallace shook his head, while Trinity raised his uninjured arm to point at him.

'You also can't count,' he said. 'Your gun's empty.'

Wallace's right eye twitched before he gathered his composure with a shrug.

'Ezra didn't fire that many times. So I can sure kill Nimrod.'

'As long as you can't harm Jessica, that's fine with me,' Nimrod said.

Jessica stood beside Nimrod, while Trinity shuffled backwards and then raised himself to a sitting position.

'You can't silence us all,' he said. 'This is over for you, Wallace. You're not an evil man, so give up without causing no more harm.'

Wallace stepped backwards towards the door. He darted his gaze between Nimrod, Jessica and Trinity as he prepared to flee, although he still kept his gun aimed at Nimrod.

Nimrod's hopes were growing that Wallace would take Trinity's advice, but then with poor timing the door opened and Haywood stepped inside. Behind him a gaggle of people was pressing forward as they came to help.

'I hope you're all fine up. . . .' Haywood said, and then tailed off when he saw the bodies on the floor.

Wallace turned to him while gesturing with the gun, so Nimrod used the distraction. He took two long steps to reach Wallace, who swirled back to face him, but he reacted too slowly, giving Nimrod enough time to slam a round-armed blow into his cheek that knocked him aside.

Wallace stumbled past the chairs until he reached the front of the box, where he thrust out a leg to stop himself. Then he stood tall and with a determined gesture aimed his gun at Nimrod, but Nimrod kept walking up to him.

He tensed expecting Wallace to fire, but then he reached him and punched his jaw, sending him reeling backwards until he tipped out of the box. A moment later a thud sounded, followed by cries of consternation.

Nimrod glanced down and winced when he saw that Wallace had fallen head first to the stage and his twisted body wouldn't be getting back up. He turned back to Jessica and shook his head, while raising a hand in a warning for her not to look down.

'I expected him to shoot,' he said.

'He did,' Jessica said. 'But either Ezra did fire six times, or there was only five bullets loaded.'

'Whatever the reason, it seems we've all got the

answers we wanted.'

Jessica nodded and came over to hug him before they moved on to help Trinity.

'So my play worked,' Haywood said as he stepped back to hold the door open.

'I guess it did,' Nimrod said. He drew Trinity to his feet. 'As I kept telling you, the truth was more effective than just making stuff up.'

Haywood shrugged. 'Maybe it was, but with your way more people died.'

CHAPTER 16

'Am I welcome in here?' Nimrod asked.

Sydney pursed his lips, suggesting he wouldn't reply. It was the early evening and Nimrod reckoned that sufficient time had passed for him to see Sydney, and promisingly Sydney was behind the bar confirming he had taken up Trinity's offer.

'All customers are welcome in the Hard Trails saloon,' Sydney muttered. He glanced at Jessica, who was standing a few paces behind Nimrod. 'Although in some cases I might make an exception.'

As Nimrod lowered his head, Jessica moved on to stand beside him.

'The fund gifted you this saloon,' she said. 'We hope you'll stay and make it a success.'

'Anyone setting up as your rival is sure to fare as badly as Oliver did,' Sydney said, addressing her for the first time that Nimrod had seen, although he didn't look her in the eye.

'I welcome having competition, and if at first it doesn't work out, the fund your father donated his legacy to will help you until you are a success.'

Sydney opened his mouth, his cold eyes suggesting he would snap back an angry retort, but he turned away with the comment left unsaid.

Jessica smiled, presumably accepting that that was the most progress she could have expected from their first conversation. Then she caught Nimrod's eye before moving down the bar to let him speak with Sydney.

'Trinity told me he spoke to you earlier,' Nimrod said. 'Are you content with his explanation of how and why your father was killed?'

'I'm pleased I have an answer, but it offers no comfort,' Sydney said. 'That goes for her behaviour and yours.'

'She did nothing wrong. It was Wallace who became jealous when she didn't return his affection. As for me, a detective has to do things he wouldn't normally do.'

Sydney sighed. 'I guess that's a lesson I should have learnt when we were at Caldwell's Stockyard.'

'Maybe, but back then I was working for someone I didn't trust. I was pleased that both my investigations here were for decent people, even if at times I doubted that.'

157

Sydney glanced at Jessica. 'Either way, if you're going to keep seeing her, you need to be careful. She's not to be trusted.'

'I'll be as careful as I've always been, although I hope you're wrong.' Nimrod shrugged. 'But if you're right, at least I'm now close to the best source of information in town.'

'She may prove useful, but as I work in the rough end of town I reckon I'll find out more useful information than she does.'

Nimrod laughed. 'That's the sort of rivalry I welcome.'

Sydney smiled, acknowledging he had been harder on Nimrod than he deserved. Then he took a deep breath and with a slow gait headed down the bar to face Jessica.

'Thank you for giving me the saloon,' he said. He raised a hand when she started to speak. 'Don't say it was owned by the fund, as Oliver told me he paid rent to you.'

'Your father would have wanted you to have it,' she said. 'Make him proud by being a success.'

'I'm not sure I want to be successful. Having money didn't help Alexander or Wallace, and you and Trinity have faced a whole heap of problems.'

'You're right, but there are many definitions of success.'

She looked around and noted a man standing at

the end of the bar hunched over a coffee. He was trail dirty and lost in his own thoughts.

Her attention made Sydney look that way and frown.

'What's interesting about him?' he asked.

'Nothing, but you ought to know his name, his business, and his problems. If he doesn't want to talk, at least he'll know that newcomers get a friendly welcome in your saloon.'

'I guess that's good advice.'

'It's more than good advice. It's what your father did when Leopold Hopeman first came in here. Clayton's hospitality made him stay, and that led to everything that's happened since, for better or for worse.'

Sydney thought for a moment and then nodded.

'Better,' he said and then moved on down the bar to stand opposite the stranger.

Nimrod watched him until the two men began chatting. Then he and Jessica headed out of the saloon and on to the main town.

'I suppose you'll be looking for a new investigation now,' she said when they were standing outside the Long Night saloon.

'I am, but that can wait,' he said. He pointed at the theatre. 'I'm meeting Haywood to tell him about my past missions. He reckons there might be a story in them.'

Jessica frowned. 'He'll have to change most of the details to protect the people involved.'

'I'm sure he won't have a problem with doing that,' Nimrod said with a laugh. 'Then again, even if he ignores the facts, all that matters is that he writes the truth.'